CW01072909

# Broomsticks and Pink Gumdrops

## A Witch's Cove Mystery
## Book 12

Vella Day

Broomsticks and Pink Gumdrops
Copyright © 2021 by Vella Day
Print Edition
www.velladay.com
velladayauthor@gmail.com

Cover Art by Jaycee DeLorenzo
Edited by Rebecca Cartee and Carol Adcock-Bezzo

Published in the United States of America

Print book ISBN: 978-1-951430-33-7

**Finding a dead body in the wall of our new candy shop was strange enough, but then someone from the past returns carrying a pink ribbon I'd left on my very strange Christmas trip to Ohio.**

As a founding member of The Pink Iguana Sleuths of Witch's Cove, I thought I'd seen it all, but I was wrong. When the sheriff's department files this as a cold case, my curiosity gets the best of me. What else is new? It also isn't helping that my talking pink iguana is insisting I look into it.

When a corpse is fairly warm, it's easy to come up with who wanted this person dead. Motives are everywhere, but not this time. We didn't even know the identity of the skeleton. I shuddered to think what kind of killer hid a body in the wall of a store? A very bad one, for sure.

Regardless of how hard it will be, Jaxson, Iggy, and I are up for the challenge. I couldn't help but wonder why an FBI agent from the past was sent to us, though. To help? Or hinder?

# Chapter One

"GUESS WHO I met?" my good friend announced with pride.

Penny Carsted and I used to waitress together at the Tiki Hut Grill. I loved it when Penny was excited. "The new owner of the yarn shop?"

"It sold? When? Have you met this person?"

I chuckled. "I hadn't heard if it has or hasn't sold. You said to guess, and I did."

"Oh, well guess again."

I had given her my one and only suggestion. "I have no idea."

"Courtney Higgins."

I had to rack my brains who that might be, but I failed to recall anyone by that name. For an amateur sleuth, it was my job to know everyone in town. Apparently, I was off my game today. "Refresh my memory who that is."

Penny laughed. "You are a hoot, Glinda."

Uh-oh. That implied I should know her. After all, Witch's Cove only had a population of two thousand. *Think.* "I got it! The new owner of the soon-to-open candy store." It was where the burned out bookstore used to be.

"Good for you."

I waited for my little gossipy friend to fill me in, but she just smiled at me. "Fine. I'll beg. Spill."

Penny was on her ten-minute break, and even though she didn't have a lot of time, she pulled out the chair across from me and sat down. "Okay. Courtney is probably in her early thirties and is really cute. I didn't want to grill her too much, but I know she's from someplace in Ohio."

"Ohio, huh? Florida will be quite the change. Did she say why she decided to open a candy store?" I don't remember the last time I'd seen one—in any town.

"I didn't ask since I didn't want to come off as being overly curious."

Like me. "I get that. Did she say when she expects her store to open?" Paper had been plastered across the windows for several days now. Considering the amount of damage from the bookstore fire, she'd have to gut the place. Since she was renting, I imagine the building owner would pay for most of the rebuilding process. On the other hand, he might not, since the owner had been on the verge of bankruptcy until the town raised money to help him out.

"No, but for your sake, I hope she opens soon." Penny knew what a sweet tooth I had.

"You and me both."

She pushed back her chair. "I'm afraid my break's over. The owner here is a tyrant."

I laughed. "For sure." That tyrant was my very lovable Aunt Fern.

"As one of the town's ambassadors, you should stop over and see if our new resident needs help with anything."

Penny just wanted to get the scoop. "So now I'm an

ambassador?"

"I thought saying you were nosy didn't sound as good."

I couldn't help but grin. "You are right. I'll see what I can find out and let you know."

Penny giggled. "You're the best."

As I finished my meal, I decided I should visit Courtney to see if I could help in some way. After all, with my connections to the town's main gossip queens, I could provide her with any information she needed. If she wanted help cleaning up, I could offer a hand, too. At the moment, my sleuth agency didn't have any customers, which meant I was free to do what I wanted.

In the past, every spare moment I had was spent waitressing in order to bring in more money to grow our company. Ever since the extremely bizarre event in which I, along with my partner, Jaxson, my cousin, Rihanna, and my familiar, Iggy, time traveled back to the 1970s for a few days over Christmas, we had more money than we needed. Long story short, we ended up being given a large substantial check.

Just as I was about to leave, my aunt came over to my table. "I see we have a new member in our community." She wiggled her eyebrows.

My Aunt Fern was one of the famous gossip ladies, mostly because one of her friends was the sheriff's grandmother, a woman who had her finger on the pulse of the town. "Did you speak with Courtney when she came in to eat?" I asked.

My aunt's eyes widened slightly. Aha. She hadn't expected I'd know that.

"I did. She is a lovely young lady."

"Besides the fact she is from Ohio, what did you learn?"

My aunt pulled out the same chair Penny had recently vacated. "She came to Witch's Cove because a fortune teller told her this was where she needed to be."

I might be a witch who believed in the talents of my fellow witches, but to move half way across the country because some fortune teller told me to wasn't something I would ever do. But what did I know about her circumstances? Nothing. "Does Courtney know anyone here?"

"Not a soul. She chose our Florida town because of its name."

I leaned forward. "Do you think that means she's a witch? I mean, why else come to Witch's Cove? She can't expect to make a killing at a candy store in a town our size." The name of her place was Broomsticks and Gumdrops, which implied she at least was open to witchcraft.

"During the high season, she'll do well."

"I hope so, but I know how much the bookstore struggled, regardless of the season."

"Candy is more popular than books these days," my aunt reminded me.

"I hope you're right."

My aunt stood. "We have to catch up."

"Totally."

She lived across the hall from me, but of late, we seemed to be ships passing in the night since our hours didn't seem to coincide.

Even though my aunt told me that my food was on the house, I always paid. After promising to give her the lowdown, I headed across the street to meet our new resident.

It was possible only workers were inside the store and not

the new owner, but if I didn't at least try to find out, I'd spend the night wondering what this Courtney Higgins person was like.

With a million questions ready, I knocked on the door's papered window. I could hear some banging inside, so when no one answered, I tried again, harder this time. And then I waited.

To my delight, a tall, beautiful brunette pulled open the door, and suddenly, I forgot what I wanted to say.

Her eyebrows rose. "Yes?"

"Hello," was about all I could get out. And trust me. I was rarely at a loss for words. What caused me to be tongue-tied, I don't know. Maybe it was that Courtney was so young and pretty.

"Can I help you?"

"Courtney?"

"Yes."

The confirmation helped me regain my composure. "I was hoping I could help you."

She smiled. "Oh! Okay. Want to come in? Just know that the place is a total mess."

*Come in* were welcome words to a curious person. "Not a problem." I stepped inside and held out my hand. "I'm Glinda Goodall. My aunt owns the Tiki Hut Grill."

"I love the food there."

"Good to hear." I debated telling her I was an amateur sleuth, but I didn't want to overwhelm her right off the bat. I looked around her construction site. Two men were ripping down the walls—walls that had dingy, water-stained wallpaper on them. "This looks like it's going to take a lot of work."

"It will, but that's why the owner isn't charging me any rent until I open. I imagine it will be another few weeks before I'm ready to install the cabinets and shelving, and then I can order the candy and other paraphernalia."

"How nice of him to give you a price break. I hope he's paying for at least some, if not all, of the renovations."

"He is."

I tried to imagine this not being a bookstore, but I couldn't. I guess I'd have to wait until she opened to see what she had in mind. "I am curious why you chose to come to Witch's Cove."

Courtney glanced to the workers and then turned back at me. "It will sound stupid."

Aha. She wanted to talk about the fortune teller. Some were legit, others were not. "Once you get to know me, you'll realize I don't think anything is out of the realm of possibility."

"Really?"

"Really."

"Come into the back so we can chat. It's not as noisy in there."

The men were making quite a racket. In the other room, she had a small table set up with a computer on top. A microwave, as well as a dorm-sized refrigerator whose face was a bit blackened no doubt as a result of the smoke damage, sat on the counter.

"Want something to drink?" she asked.

"I'm good."

Courtney grabbed a soda out of her small fridge and sat down. "My story is strange sounding, even to me. First though, let me give you a brief history of the life of Courtney Higgins." She smiled.

"I'm all ears."

"I was engaged to this really great guy—or at least I thought he was a great guy until he found another woman and told me he didn't think having an entrepreneur for a girlfriend was a good thing. When he dumped me, I'm not proud to say I kind of went on an emotional rollercoaster."

"Who wouldn't?" Jaxson was the first real boyfriend I'd had. If he decided he didn't want to be with me, I wasn't sure how I would cope.

"Right? Anyway, about three weeks after the breakup, I was with a few of my friends who convinced me to go to this local fair. It was a hokey little thing, but I knew there would be great fudge—something I can never say no to."

My heart zinged, and then I moaned. "I love homemade fudge."

When our town had a save-this-strip-of-buildings fundraiser, Jaxson bought me some of the rich, chocolatey confection, which I thought was such a romantic gesture. That fair, especially its Ferris wheel ride, made for such a memorable day.

"Me, too. After we gorged on it, we saw this fortune teller. I wasn't going to have a session, but this woman told one of my friends a few things that were so dead on about her life that I had to give her a try."

"She told you to come to Witch's Cove?"

"Not exactly. She said that the only way to find true love was to leave behind the life I had and start anew."

I whistled. I believed in true love, so I couldn't tell her she was being foolish, but to move to a new town because someone suggested it? Even I wouldn't do that, and I've been tempted to do quite a lot of crazy things in my twenty-seven years. "I'm not sure I could pack up and leave my family."

"My parents were killed three years ago in a car accident, and I was an only child."

My heart cracked. "I am so sorry."

Her lips pressed together. "Thanks."

A change of topic was clearly needed. "Why Florida?"

"Have you ever been to Ohio in the winter?" she asked and then chuckled.

"I have. Once. I thought it was so beautiful when it snowed, but I understand that the cold might get old after a while. If this fortune teller suggested Florida, why Witch's Cove?" I was wondering if Courtney's story would match what she'd told Aunt Fern.

"The truth? I loved the name."

I really wanted to ask if she was a witch, but I thought that was a bit too forward for having just met her. Not all witches were comfortable with their talents being known.

"If you ever want more hints about your future, we have the Psychics Corner right down the street. I can personally vouch for several of the people being authentic."

"You're saying they are actual witches?"

Her hint of surprise kind of implied she wasn't one. "Yup. Mind you I've never asked for a love spell or anything, but they have been able to contact the dead for me."

"For real?"

I might as well come clean. "My partner, Jaxson Harrison, and I run an amateur sleuth business. I bring it up because the person who knows the most about the murder is often the dead person." That wasn't always the case, but it was sometimes.

She stilled. "You're serious, aren't you?"

"As the day is long." Sheesh. Who said that anymore? I must be hanging out with the gossip queens too much.

I didn't feel comfortable enough to tell her that I'd seen ghosts and spoken with them. Nor would I mention I had a talking pink iguana who was my familiar since only witches had familiars.

"Maybe I'll see if I can talk to my parents then." Her bottom chin trembled. "Once I get settled, that is."

I couldn't imagine what life would be like without mine. "I bet it could help." I cleared my throat, needing a second to think of a something different to say. "So, do you have an artist's rendition of how you envision your store?"

Courtney seemed to shake herself out of her reminiscing too. "I do."

She pushed back her chair, opened one of the soot-stained cabinets, and retrieved a rolled up piece of paper. "The real items I purchase may be different than this artist's sketch, but this will show you my vision."

When she unrolled it, I sucked in a breath. Looking at the vibrant colors and the massive amount of candy spiked my blood sugar. "Wow. That looks awesome."

"You think?" I nodded. She then tapped the paper. "In this corner, I want to have some Witch's Cove souvenirs, like T-shirts and stuff, for the tourists."

We have several stores that sold that kind of gear. "Since the name of your store is Broomsticks and Gumballs, why not sell witch stuff?"

"I guess I could. What do you think would sell?"

I didn't want her to compete too much with Hex and Bones Apothecary, but there were things that could be unique to her store. "Some small cauldrons, incense, and of course, small witchy broomsticks."

She grinned. "That's a great idea."

It was, wasn't it? Since the space was rather large, I wanted to offer another suggestion. "Have you thought of having a counter where you serve sodas and such? People might want to come here for a date night. We have an ice cream shop in town, but that's about all."

"I'll definitely think about it."

The noise in the other room suddenly stopped. A moment later, someone knocked on the door, and a worker peeked his head in. "Ah, Miss Higgins?"

"Yes?"

"Sorry to bother you, but you gotta see this."

The worker's expression, along with his shaking hand, made me think he'd seen a ghost. We jumped up and dashed into the room where they'd finished tearing apart a partitioned wall. That in and of itself was not disturbing, but what took my breath away was what was inside the wall.

Courtney moved closer and then faced the worker. "Is that what I think it is?"

"Yes, ma'am. Should we call the sheriff?"

Courtney looked over at me. "Glinda?"

"I'll run over to the sheriff's department and let Steve know."

And here I thought I'd seen it all.

# Chapter Two

"THANK YOU." COURTNEY stepped back and placed a hand over her mouth. "Please hurry."

"I will." I ran down the sidewalk—which wasn't a pretty sight—and dashed into the sheriff's office, which was three storefronts away.

The deputy, Nash Solano, was at his desk. I must have looked really scared, or maybe a better term was scary, because he jumped up and rushed toward me. "What happened?"

"Courtney Higgins, the new candy store owner, just found a skeleton in her wall."

"What?"

I thought I'd made myself clear. "There is a skeleton in the wall of her candy shop."

Nash dashed back to his desk, picked up a few things, and then returned. "Show me."

I'm sure Pearl, the sheriff's grandmother and station receptionist, was in too much shock to ask a question, but I bet it wouldn't take long before the whole town knew about the hidden body.

We walked and jogged back to the store, though I didn't know why we had to hurry. The skeleton wasn't going anywhere. When we entered the shop, Courtney and the two workers moved to the side.

"Did anyone touch the body?" Nash asked, sounding like the professional that he was.

"No." Courtney's voice trembled.

I stepped up next to my new friend—if I could be so bold as to call her that—and craned my neck to see around Nash who was bending over the pile of bones.

"What's he or she wearing?" I whispered my question to Courtney since I didn't want to disturb the deputy's concentration.

The hair was shoulder length, so I couldn't say for sure what the sex might have been. The shirt was in tatters, and the jeans were…well, jeans that kind of looked like bell bottoms. The fact the person was wearing sneakers like my Converses also confused me.

"Not something you'd find in today's stores," she said.

Nash turned around. "I trust no one knows who this guy might be, right?" We all shook our heads. He pulled out his phone, no doubt calling the medical examiner. After he spoke with Dr. Sanchez, aka his girlfriend, he pocketed his phone. "I'm afraid I'm going to have to ask all of you to leave."

Courtney appeared crestfallen, and I couldn't blame her. This store was her dream. "Why? I have a lot of work to do."

"I know that, but this is a crime scene. I'm not expecting the medical examiner to take more than an hour or two."

Poor Courtney looked so upset. "Can you call me when I can return?"

"Of course." Nash took her number.

She sighed heavily. "Is there any way you can keep this quiet? I don't want this to affect my business." She shook her head. "Who wants to come to a candy store where a body had been stuffed in a wall?"

Nash nodded, his lips pressed together in sympathy. "I'll see what I can do."

It was a shame that Pearl already heard me announce the presence of the skeleton. Soon she'd be telling everyone about the novel news. I turned to Courtney. "Want to grab something at the diner? You shouldn't be alone right now."

Her shoulders sagged. "That would be wonderful."

I didn't envy Nash having to deal with this, but at least the bones didn't smell. If the body had been in the wall since before Frank and Betty Sanchez had their store, they would be really old. I refused to believe the previous occupants had killed anyone and then hidden the corpse, never expecting the wall to be removed. I shivered at that morbid thought.

Courtney and I crossed the street and headed south to the diner. "I should warn you that the owner, Dolly Andrews, is a fabulous woman, but she has a tendency to gossip." I chuckled. "Who am I kidding? She and several other women—including my aunt—live for gossip. Tell Dolly, tell the whole town."

"I bet that comes in handy sometimes when you're look-ing for clues for a case."

I was impressed with Courtney's quick thinking. "You are so right. Dolly has helped us solve many a crime. Two of the other chatty ladies are the owners of the tea shop and coffee shop. They are twin spinsters. Then there is the sheriff's grandmother who works as his receptionist." I didn't want to assume that Pearl had blabbed yet, though that was most likely the case.

Courtney partially smiled. "Thanks for the tip."

We entered the diner and snagged a table. "The shakes are wonderful here, but all of their food is good."

"Thanks for the tip." Courtney studied the menu. When she'd decided, she leaned back. "You said it was a bookstore that burned down?"

"Yes. Frank and Betty Sanchez ran it for as long as I can remember."

"How old is the building?"

"That's an excellent question. I don't know, but it should be easy enough to find out." Since I had communicated with the buildings' owner on many occasions, I pulled out my phone to contact him.

"Glinda?"

"Yes, it's me. I have a question for you. How old is your building?"

"How old? Hmm. I think it was built about fifty years ago. My dad, of course, would have known the exact date. Why?"

His father had recently passed away. "Just curious. I'm having something to eat with the new candy store owner."

"Courtney. We've met. What's this really about, Glinda?"

Shoot. I thought I was being circumspect. I should have asked Courtney if she minded if I told the building owner about the body. After all, he had a right to know. I mouthed that it was Heath Richards. "Can I tell him?" I whispered.

"Sure."

"Please keep this under wraps, but there was an incident." I told him about the body.

"A body? How long do you think it's been there?"

"I don't know, but the remains are now a skeleton, which would mean a long time."

He whistled. "Thanks. I'll talk to the sheriff about it."

"Good plan." I hung up and then turned to Courtney. "As you probably heard, Heath knew nothing about any skeleton."

"What about the former owners?"

"I can certainly speak with them." I looked up and spotted Dolly coming toward us. "Here comes the owner. Be prepared for questions."

Courtney nodded. "I'm ready."

"Glinda, who's your friend?"

I introduced them. Naturally, Dolly welcomed her to Witch's Cove and then proceeded to basically interrogate her. I had to hand it to our newcomer. She probably decided she'd told the fortune teller story enough times and wisely chose not to mention it. As to why she chose Witch's Cove? She used the tried and true reason of wanting better weather.

"It's nice to meet you, Courtney. What can I get you two ladies to eat?"

I went with a glass of sweet tea since I'd just eaten, but Courtney chose a more nutritious meal of a ham and cheese sandwich. Once Dolly took off, Courtney's eyes widened. "I can see what you mean. I'll have to watch what I say."

"Yes, but Dolly and her friends can be useful, especially once you open. You'll need help spreading the word about your new business, and no one is better than our gossip queens."

"It would be awesome to get some free publicity."

"Totally." I wasn't sure what else to talk about since the

dead body topic was off the table. There were too many ears nearby. If she'd just moved here, Courtney had nothing to do with this man's death. "Where are you living?"

"I'm renting a place on the edge of town. It's temporary until I get on my feet."

"If you stop at the coffee shop, Miriam is friends with several realtors."

"Thanks. So, tell me about yourself," she said.

Me? I was used to asking the questions, but it was only fair, I guess, to tell her about myself. "I'm from here. My parents own the funeral home and, as I said, the Tiki Hut Grill belongs to my aunt." I told her about having tried my hand at teaching math and then waitressing, when I decided to open an amateur sleuth agency with my boyfriend, Jaxson Harrison.

"That is fascinating. Do you have a background in law enforcement?" she asked.

I suppose my witch talents would be discovered soon enough. "No. I'm just nosy, and I'm a witch—which comes in handy at times."

She laughed. "A witch? You're kidding, right?"

While Courtney's words said one thing, her tone wasn't filled with disbelief. Interesting. "Nope."

"What can you do?"

"A little of this and a little of that." I listed a few of the spells I'd done, including being able to cloak myself, but that was a long time ago—or so it seemed.

"I'm impressed." Courtney leaned forward. "Can you move things with your mind?"

I had moved small things, but it wasn't more than half an

inch. "Not consistently."

"I'm honored to meet you."

We then chatted a bit more about her boyfriend and why that relationship had crumbled, since the topic of the occult seemed to be closed.

"I don't think men like successful women," she finally said.

"That's not true. Jaxson, my partner, loves that we have a business together."

"Aw, that is sweet. I should have said that Dan didn't like powerful women." Her face turned pink at having given herself that label. That said something about her, but I wasn't quite sure what.

"Roger that."

"How did you and Jaxson meet?"

I didn't want to tell her what a bad boy he'd been and give her the wrong impression. Jaxson became a totally different person once he'd been acquitted of a crime he didn't commit. "His brother, Drake, and I went to school together, and we are best friends. Drake owns the wine and cheese shop across the street."

"I'll have to check it out."

"You should. It's awesome."

We'd just finished our meal when Courtney's phone rang. "Oh, it's the deputy." She answered it. "Yes?" Courtney gave me a thumbs up. "Great. Thank you."

"Did Nash give you the all-clear?" I asked.

"He did. Thank you for giving up your time to keep me company."

"Thank you for being so open and welcoming. If you

need anything, call me." I handed her my business card.

After we paid, we went our separate ways. I went straight to our office since I wanted to tell Jaxson and Iggy the news. I had to be prepared that Jaxson wouldn't be there. He might not have come in today since we didn't have anything on the docket. However, cases always popped up when we weren't expecting them, so maybe he had.

When I opened the door, Rihanna was there instead. "I didn't expect to find you here. I thought you were spending the day with Gavin." She lived in the spare room in back.

Rihanna, my eighteen-year-old cousin had just graduated from high school last weekend and was spending her days taking pictures and enjoying life with her boyfriend, Gavin, who was studying to be a doctor. Lucky for him, he was the medical examiner's son. Only then did it dawn on me that he would be with his mom. "Of course. The body. Did Gavin tell you about it?"

She sat on the sofa and motioned I join her. "Only that it was his mom's first skeleton. Nash said you'd reported the body?"

Ah, yes, life in a small town. "I did."

"So? I want the details."

Rihanna might not know it, but I bet my witchy cousin would end up being a sleuth one day. She was talented, especially since she had a knack for reading minds. I looked around. "Have you seen Jaxson?"

"No."

"Let me call him so I don't have to tell the rather interesting story twice." Or three times if Iggy wasn't here. "Iggy, you around?"

He popped his head out of the small, makeshift kitchen. "You called?"

I laughed. "I have some gossip to impart, but first I want to find Jaxson."

"He's downstairs with his brother."

"Thank you." I turned to Rihanna. "How about joining me downstairs? That way Drake won't have to leave the store."

She jumped up. "Sure."

"You just going to leave me here?" Iggy asked.

I smiled. "Never."

I picked up my nine-pound snoop and headed down the interior staircase where I could hear Jaxson laughing. I debated not breaking up the brother bonding time, but this news was important.

With Rihanna right behind me, we entered the store's back room. Jaxson looked up and smiled. "You look excited."

"I am." A mysterious death had a way of turning a bad day into a good one. "You won't believe what happened."

Jaxson patted the chair next to his. "Tell me."

I placed Iggy on the table while Rihanna sat next to Drake. I had to assume that Drake's girlfriend, Andorra, was manning the Hex and Bones store today. Of late, when they weren't working, the two of them were always together.

"I met the new owner of the candy store," I announced.

Jaxson's chin jutted forward a bit. "And?"

He knew me well. I went through what Penny and my aunt told me about her and then what Courtney herself divulged. "The workers had taken down the face of one of the walls when they found a skeleton stuffed inside."

`

Iggy spun around. "A skeleton? I want to see it."

"There's nothing to see but a bunch of bones."

"You don't understand. I bet he doesn't stink anymore."

I chuckled. Iggy hated the stench of death, and I couldn't blame him. "We'll see. For now, our mystery person is with Dr. Sanchez and Gavin."

"Any idea who he might be?" Drake asked.

I explained about the tattered clothes and longish hair. "Considering the body is a skeleton, it must be rather old."

"Do you think Frank Sanchez knows anything?" Jaxson asked.

"That's exactly who I plan to speak with next. As the former owner, he might be privy to some gossip. Do you want to come with me?"

Jaxson wrapped an arm around my shoulder. "I'd love nothing better, pink lady."

"Rihanna, Drake?"

"I have to work," Drake said.

"I'll pass," my cousin replied.

"Don't look at me. I'm staying with Rihanna," Iggy said.

Visiting Betty and Frank probably wasn't all that appealing. "Suit yourselves."

# Chapter Three

"DON'T YOU THINK we should have called Frank and Betty first to let them know we were stopping by?" Jaxson asked as I pulled up in front of their home.

"Maybe, but we're here now." I smiled sweetly. The real answer was yes, I should have, but I was so excited to find out what they knew that I'd lost my manners.

Jaxson and I piled out of the car. Hopefully, the former bookstore owners were home. I knocked, and about thirty seconds later, Betty answered.

"Glinda, Jaxson. This is a surprise."

I couldn't tell if she was happy for the company or not. The fact our visit was a surprise, though, implied no one from the sheriff's department had spoken with them. Either Nash was waiting for Steve to return from wherever he had been, before contacting them, or else, the deputy didn't think they had anything to do with the man's death.

"May we come in?" I asked.

"Sure. Of course. I'll tell Frank you are here. Come sit down."

We took a seat on the sofa. A moment later, Frank showed up. "How nice to see you two."

I was thrilled to hear him sounding so cheerful. We chatted a bit about what he'd been doing to keep busy until Betty returned with a tray of iced tea. It was my favorite drink, but Jaxson didn't drink sugar, as he liked to say. However, he grabbed a glass and thanked her.

"What brings you here?" Betty asked.

I told them about the skeleton found in the wall of the old bookstore, and to say the least, they were shocked. "You had no idea it was there, I take it?"

"No! How old do you think the body is?" Frank asked.

"I don't know. Old." I couldn't even fathom a guess, though the body was garbed in clothes that screamed of the sixties or seventies.

"The skeleton would have to have died more than thirty years ago since we started our bookstore in the nineties," Betty said.

"When was the building built?" The owner hadn't been sure. If they didn't know, I could look in the courthouse records.

Betty looked at her husband who waved a hand. "I think maybe twenty years older than that. I honestly don't remember."

"Heath Richards' father must have been really young when he built it."

"I imagine he was."

We caught up on any good books they'd been reading, and Betty rattled off a few names. As nice as it was to catch up with them, we had other things to do, and they probably did, too. I stood. "I'll let you know if we find out anything, assuming you want to know."

"Of course," Frank said. "It is a bit creepy thinking we

worked in a store that housed a dead body all those years, but I am curious how it got there."

I couldn't imagine learning I'd worked beside a dead person all those years either. "Me too."

I hugged the couple goodbye, and then we left. Once in the car, I faced Jaxson. "I don't know what I expected, but I was hoping for more."

"I know. Now what?" Jaxson asked.

"I'm not sure. There's not much we can do since we don't know the identity of the person. Even if by some chance we learn who it is, whoever killed him or her could be dead by now or no longer living in town."

Jaxson stared at me. "Are you telling me that you're going to let it drop?"

Was that what I was saying? "Nah. It's not in my genes." I flashed him a smile. "I want to see if Gertrude has a clue. She lived here since the dawn of time. I wouldn't be surprised if she was around when the building was being constructed."

"You should stop by, but how about taking Rihanna with you, assuming she's free. My brother and I still have some brainstorming to do."

Brainstorming? Did he plan to work with Drake on the case without me? "About what?"

"How to make more money for his store."

That was a relief. "I'm sure he'll appreciate his older brother's wisdom."

Jaxson barked out a laugh. "I'm not sure about that, but he does listen to all good suggestions."

I parked in front of the office and headed upstairs to speak with Rihanna while Jaxson went downstairs to his brother's shop.

"How did it go?" my cousin asked.

I told her what little they knew. "I'm hoping Gertrude will know something. Want to come?"

She grinned. "I'm always up for seeing my favorite psychic."

I didn't even ask Iggy if he wanted to join us since I knew what he'd say. I scooped him up. "Gertrude would love to see you."

He lifted his tiny head. "That's because I'm awesome."

I really needed to work on his humility. I probably should have called first, but should she have a client, I was willing to wait until she was free. When the three of us arrived, we only had to sit for about twenty minutes.

Once we were told to go back to her office, I knocked on Gertrude's door. When I stuck my head in, she looked up from her desk and smiled. "Glinda! Please come in. I didn't see your name on the …"

"That's because I just came over for a quick chat about something that happened."

She looked over at Rihanna. Since my cousin had trained under Gertrude, they were probably trying to read each other's minds. It wasn't exactly communicating telepathically, but I bet it was close.

"Yes, I heard about the skeleton." Gertrude seemed to know about that without either of us having said a word out loud. "How strange. Are you taking this case?" Gertrude turned her attention back to me.

"Maybe." Rihanna and I sat down. I lifted Iggy out of my purse and placed him on the table.

"Hi, Ms. Poole," he said.

She smiled. "Iggy, I told you to call me Gertrude."

So now he had manners? He could be such a little stinker. "Thanks, *Gertrude*," he said.

"As far as taking the case, at the moment, there is no case," I said. "We don't even know who this person is, which is why we are here." Most likely she already knew that. "I was wondering if you heard anything about a missing person case many years ago—like fifty years ago."

She looked off to the side. "Not that I recall, but let me think about it. It might take me a while to sort through all of my memories."

I didn't want to pressure her. "No rush. I have another question. Do you remember when the strip of stores across the street was built?" I would think the skeleton would have to have been walled up during the initial stage of development.

"The year? Not really, but I'm thinking around 1970 or so."

"Thanks, that gives us a good time frame to do research."

"Us?" Gertrude asked.

I chuckled. "Jaxson and I have no cases at the moment, so I thought I'd see if I can at least learn who this mystery person is."

She smiled. "I hope you do."

We spent a few more minutes discussing her health and how things were going in the psychic world. When her cell beeped indicating she had another appointment, we excused ourselves.

Once outside, I turned to Rihanna. "I gather she wasn't hiding anything?"

"Gertrude always keeps a few things back, but all in all, she was honest."

"I'm happy to hear that."

When we returned to the office, I wasn't sure what I should work on. Without a name to the body, there wasn't much I could do. To my delight, though, Jaxson was sitting at his desk. I placed Iggy on the floor and dropped down next to Jaxson as Rihanna went back to her room. "What are you working on?"

"Nothing much. I just wanted to see if there were any articles about any missing person in Witch's Cove way back when."

"Find anything?"

He laughed. "I'm good, but I'm not that good. Remember, the Internet wasn't around back then."

"I keep forgetting. This reminds me of when we time traveled back to Ohio, and we had no cell phones and no computers."

He faced me. "How did we manage to solve that murder?"

"Good old fashioned detective work."

Iggy's feet scraped across the floor. "Don't forget how I helped."

He had basically solved the crime. It might have been sort of dumb luck to have stepped on a diamond, but he figured things out, nonetheless. "You're right." I turned back to Jaxson. "Maybe we can find something at the library."

"Maybe."

When he didn't move, I figured he wanted to exhaust the computer search first. "What happens when we do learn who this person is?"

"I don't know, but I like a good mystery." Jaxson winked. That was usually my line.

"How about I give Delilah a call? I bet she'd love something to dig her teeth into. Figuring out a murder case would be really exciting to her."

"Go right ahead."

I pulled out my phone and called my friend who worked at the library.

"Glinda! Nice to hear from you."

"You, too." We had caught up a few weeks ago, but if I worked on a case, I rarely had the time to go out with my friends. "I was wondering if maybe you could do a little research for me."

"I'd love to. It's been rather slow around here."

I told Delilah about the body that was found and the approximate time of death. "I could be off by ten years or more."

"Ooh, that sounds exciting. I'll get right on it, but a fifty-year-old article will take me a couple of days to research."

"No rush"

"I'm looking forward to checking into this. Do you know the skeleton's approximate age?"

"Not yet, but I'm hoping our medical examiner can give us an idea. I'll let you know if I find out any details."

"Great," she said. "We'll be in touch."

I disconnected, feeling quite satisfied and turned back to Jaxson. "That was easy."

He chuckled. "And if Delilah comes up empty-handed?"

I punched him lightly. "Let me bask in my brilliance for a

few hours at least."

He leaned over and kissed my forehead. "You do that. Right now, I need to keep looking."

The person who would know the most about the skeleton would be Elissa Sanchez, the medical examiner. While she'd only received the body a little while ago, she should be able to tell the body's sex and approximate age, right? Busting into her morgue and asking questions might not be well-received, but a phone call from her son's girlfriend might help pave the way.

I knocked on Rihanna's bedroom door.

"Come in."

I stepped inside. "Since I'm an impatient person—"

"You don't say."

"Smarty pants. Do you think you could ask Gavin if his mother has any idea what the sex and age of the skeleton might be?"

"Because?"

I explained that Jaxson was trying to research the person's identity. "Considering when the building was constructed, combined with what he or she was wearing, I'm thinking the person was killed fifty or so years ago, but knowing if it is a male or not would help."

She smiled. "I can ask. Gavin texted a while ago that he was learning a lot about bones."

"That's great. You're going to miss him when he goes off to college, aren't you?"

Rihanna glanced to the ceiling. "He'll only be two hours away. Gavin said he'd come home on the weekends if he could."

"That's great." I would not warn her how hard long-distance relationships could be, but if any two people could make it work, it would be those two.

She pulled out her phone and called her boyfriend. It took a lot less convincing than I thought it would. Once Rihanna finished, she faced me. "His mom is struggling. As you saw, the bones aren't attached to each other like they are in a science class mannequin. However, the pelvis indicates it's a male. That part was easy. The teeth were in good shape, which helped with identifying age. She put him at about forty-five."

"Thank you. I guess the next step is to figure out if the body was stuffed in a wall during the initial build."

Rihanna's brows furrowed. "Don't you think the workers would have noticed a body in the wall when they covered the studs with sheetrock or whatever they used?"

She had a point. "Yes, unless one of the workers was the killer."

"Ooh, I like it. What's next?"

I told her that Delilah was doing a little digging. "I'll let her know we are looking for a forty-five-year-old male."

"Perfect."

I texted my friend the information, hoping it would help. Once that was done, I returned to the living room. "Any luck?"

"Nope."

"Rihanna found out that our mystery person is a forty-five year old male."

"Thank you. That will help.

Now what should I do next?

# Chapter Four

SINCE JAXSON WASN'T able to find any further information about the skeleton, despite knowing his age, I opted not to go into work the next day. Instead, I went for a walk on the beach, which was something I rarely did. Working on a case had a way of eating away all of my free time. Usually, we at least had some small job, even if it was merely following a wayward spouse, but not at the moment. All we had was a mysterious skeleton.

I contemplated bugging the deputy about whether he'd made any progress on the missing person's case, but since I had nothing to offer him in return, I decided to mind my own business for a change.

Just as I finished showering from my rather hot beach walk, my cell rang. I thought it might be Jaxson suggesting we take in a movie and then have dinner, but to my surprise, it was Dr. Sanchez.

"Hey, Elissa. Did you find something?" I was hoping she'd have figured out the cause of the skeleton's death.

"I'm afraid not. The bones aren't really telling me anything. As you saw, there were no organs to check. If the person was poisoned, I can't tell, and the bones showed no sign of trauma."

That wasn't good. "Do you have any idea how long he was in the wall?"

"Not with any precision, and I don't have the equipment to do much testing. I can tell you he broke his arm twice as a child. From the spiral nature of the break, it was due to abuse. He did, however, take good care of his teeth, despite having had a lot of cavities. He might have grown up in a time before fluoride was prevalent in the water."

"That might help narrow down his identity. Thanks."

"That's not why I called, though," she rushed on to say.

I stilled "Do you need my help with something?"

"Actually, I do. Even though I found nothing to indicate cause of death, it is highly unlikely that he died from natural causes. Otherwise, he wouldn't have been stuffed in the wall."

"I have to agree with you."

"All I could conclude was that he had surprisingly strong bones, so I imagine he was a powerful man."

Dr. Sanchez was beating around the bush for a reason. "Would you like me to give my necklace a try?"

Of late, it seemed as if my witch skills were needed more and more. To be honest, I wasn't sure it would help. My magical pendant, when swung over a deceased body, could often detect the cause of death. Over a pile of bones, I had no idea.

"That would be great if you could. I figure we have nothing to lose."

In other words, I couldn't do worse than coming up empty-handed. "I'm free now." Though my visit might necessitate another shower since Iggy hated any remnants of death on me.

"Super. Come over when it's convenient."

As soon as I hung up, I called Jaxson and gave him the rundown.

"Call me when you are done. Drake and I are in the middle of something, or I'd come with you. We can do dinner when you get back if you like."

"I'd love that." I was always happy when we were together.

I told Iggy my plans, not bothering to ask if he wanted to come with me since I was well aware how much he really disliked the morgue.

"I'll stay here, or else I'll go for a walk."

"I figured." He'd either see Aimee, his cat girlfriend, or head over to the office.

After I threw on some rather tattered, casual clothes, I drove to the morgue.

When I entered, Gavin was in the main area. "I'm glad you're here. Mom is pretty frustrated. I don't think she's worked on a lot of bones before."

"I don't imagine most medical examiners have." Other than when they were studying to be doctors. "Can I go in?"

"Yes." Gavin tapped the door code and motioned me inside.

The room didn't smell bad for a change. I suppose without flesh, the corpse wouldn't stink.

"Oh, good. You're here." Elissa sounded a bit flustered.

On the table was a pile of bones that I guess were placed in more or less anatomical order. The skull was at the top and the pelvis sat in the middle. Other than that, I just saw bones. "Not much to go on, is it?"

"No, but your necklace has done wondrous things in the past."

I might need some divine intervention for this to work. As I lifted my arms to unhook my necklace, Elissa's eyes widened. "Glinda, your necklace."

"Give me a sec. I'm taking it off."

"No. It's glowing yellow."

I stilled and then looked down at the stone. What had been a pink gem was now flashing a light amber color. That had happened only one other time, and that was when I was in the presence of a rather evil warlock. Hoping there was some mistake, I removed my necklace and held it over the bones.

I waited for the color to change, but the pulses remained the same hue and saturation. Probably to make myself feel like I'd actually done something, I swung my pendant across the pile, starting at where I presumed the feet were located and slowly traveled upward. I thought the color might change to purple when I reached the pelvis to indicate poison, or to green when I dangled it over where the heart might have been, but without any organs, it didn't happen. From toes to the top of the head, nothing changed.

"I can't be positive, but I'd have to say someone with magic killed him."

"Any idea how?"

I was not the scientist. She was. "You saw the pendant remain yellow the whole time. All I can say is that magic was involved. Keep in mind, it's possible I'm wrong since I've never used my necklace on just bones before."

Elissa nodded. "I understand. What about Andorra? She

could sense things the last time she looked at a body."

"I don't know the full extent of her capabilities, but give her a call." I told Elissa Andorra's number. "I believe she's at the store, but I imagine she could stop by after work."

"Thank you."

"Other than the sex and age of this person, do you know anything else?" I didn't want to embarrass her, but I wanted to know how close we were to finding this person's identity.

"No, but like I said, that's mostly because I don't have the tools here to do the job."

I wonder if she thought some of her friends in Miami could help her. "What are you going to do?"

"I plan to take the skull to Tampa in the hopes they can do a 3-D scan of the skull. I know someone who does clay reconstruction there. If we have a face, we might get lucky and find someone who recognizes this man."

"Can you find out when he died?"

"Yes, by carbon-14 dating the bones. I'll take a sample and send it off to a lab right away."

That sounded promising. "How long will this all take?"

Elissa drew in her bottom lip. "That is hard to say. A week to several months, depending on how backlogged their labs are. I doubt anyone will consider this a high-profile case."

"No, I guess not. Thanks for taking this seriously."

She tucked in her chin. "I take all of my cases seriously."

"I'm sorry. I know, but if this John Doe has been dead for forty or more years, the relatives might have grown tired of asking for updates on finding this man."

She rubbed my arm. "Sad to say, you're probably right."

A bit embarrassed, I cleared my throat. "Thanks for asking me to help."

"Are you kidding? Thank you."

I don't know how learning that witchcraft was involved actually helped her find out how he'd died, but I'm glad Elissa believed I had aided her in some way. It would be better if Andorra could pinpoint the type of magic. Then, it would be Steve and Nash's responsibility to find the identity of the person and the name of the killer.

I left, a bit discouraged that it would take at least a week or more to get any answers. It had already been two days since this man was found in the walls of Courtney's store, and I wondered if Steve had any leads.

Instead of going back to my apartment and getting ready for my dinner date, I crossed the street and entered the sheriff's department. Pearl, who finished work around three, had already left. In her place was Jennifer Larson.

"Hey, Glinda. I heard you had quite the shock the other day."

Usually, Jennifer wasn't the gossipy type, but most likely Pearl had filled her in—or else Nash and Steve had mentioned the skeleton. "I did. I've never seen a real skeleton before."

"Any idea who it is?"

"Nope. I'm hoping Nash or Steve have learned something."

"Nash is running down some things, but Steve is in his office. Go on back."

"Thanks."

As I walked past Nash's desk, I could hear Jennifer say something to our sheriff—most likely telling him I was about to descend on him. When I entered, Steve was pulling out his yellow note pad from his top desk drawer. Uh-oh. That implied he thought I had news for him. If he'd spoken with Dr. Sanchez, he'd know what I knew.

"Glinda. Always nice to see you. Have a seat."

That was a strange greeting. "Thanks. What's wrong?"

"Nothing. I just got off the phone with Elissa."

Then he knew everything I did. "Besides the skeleton's age and general health, did the information help?"

"Not really. I'm not sure even Elissa's friend's reconstruction will lead to the man's identity. From what our competent medical examiner said, it happened quite some time ago."

Something was up with him. "Did she also mention that magic might have caused his death."

"She did."

I waited for him to say he'd like my help, but he leaned back in his chair, and I was unsure why he was playing this game. "And?"

He placed his elbows on the desk. "This is going to sound rather unorthodox, but how would you like to help me with this case?" He held up a hand. "Mind you, this is not in any official capacity. If you learn anything, you'd be required to pass it by me."

I had to laugh. "You want me to do your work for you?"

Steve planted a hand on his chest. "Glinda, like you've often reminded me, I am not qualified to deal with all this witch stuff. I've always deferred to you, but for your information, I did a little research. I just wasn't able to find any record of a missing person from fifty years ago that matches this man's age and height. And trust me, I looked through every file. Let me tell you, it was no easy chore. The records were a mess."

"I'm sorry to hear that. If you just learned a few hours ago that the skeleton was a male, how much work could you have done?" Okay, that was a bit snarky, but I was frustrated. I shouldn't be taking it out on him.

He shook his head. "I was open to male or female, and to any adult age. I found no record of a missing person case fifty years ago. Period. So will you help?"

"Fine, but only because I have no other case on the docket."

"Great." He grinned. "And good luck."

"Thank you."

Since I still had time before my date with Jaxson, I thought I'd stop by the candy store and let Courtney know what we'd learned. Even though she had nothing to do with the person's death, it probably wouldn't matter much to her who this skeleton was, but it might be something to tell her customers at some point.

When I walked to her store, I saw that paper was still covering the windows. I tried the doorknob and found it unlocked, so I stuck my head in. "Hello?"

Workers had replaced all of the wallboard and had put one coat of paint on the walls. As I studied the transformation, Courtney came out from the back room.

"Oh, hey. I thought I heard someone out here." She smiled. "Thank goodness it's you."

What did that mean? "Yeah, sorry about being MIA, but I've been trying to track down the identity of your *visitor*."

"Learn anything?"

"A little."

"Come on into the back."

"Your shop is really shaping up," I said.

She smiled. "They are doing a great job."

Once seated in the back, she offered me a drink, and this time, I accepted a bottle of tea. "I met with the medical examiner," I said.

"Oh, really? What did she tell you?"

I told Courtney the man's approximate age and that he was in good shape. I then explained about my magical pink pendant and how it glowed yellow even before I took it off. "That has only happened one other time. It was when I was in the presence of a bad warlock."

"Ouch. I'd love to hear that story—but at a later time. I really need this skeleton thing cleared up ASAP." Her lips pursed.

"What's wrong?"

"When I moved here, I knew that small towns would be challenging, but there has been a non-stop parade of people wanting to see where the skeleton was found."

"I can't say I'm surprised. That's very much a Witch's Cove thing. I don't remember if we've ever had a skeleton found in a wall before. It's a novelty."

Courtney sipped her drink. "At first I thought it was a good thing since it meant people would at least be aware of the new store going in."

"But?"

"Too many said they would never shop here knowing a dead body had been in the wall."

"That is ridiculous and narrow-minded of them. It's not as if you knew he was there." I waved a hand. "Don't worry.

They'll get over it."

"I hope you're right."

Someone knocked on the door, and a man stuck his head in. "John and I are leaving, but we'll be back in the morning."

"Thanks, and goodnight."

How terrible for Courtney to suffer because of what someone else did so long ago. "I'm sure that when everyone sees what an amazing place this is, they'll forget all about that poor man."

She chuckled. "Let's hope. Maybe I should hang a skeleton up in the corner and place a sign over it saying it was the elephant in the room."

I grinned. "I think that is brilliant, but what would be even cooler, would be to put a fake skeleton sticking out of the wall, like he's trying to escape. It would go with the witch theme."

Courtney laughed. "That would draw a lot of attention—hopefully, good attention. I'll certainly think about it."

"I bet it would stop the idle tongues. Throw in some other witchy stuff and you'll be good to go."

She smiled. "I like it."

We talked a bit more about how she was finding small town life other than the busy bodies who'd stopped by. Since I wasn't sure what time Jaxson and I would be going out to dinner, I told her I had to get back. I needed to clean up before I shared my day with my partner.

When I stepped into my apartment, Iggy wasn't there. Oh, well. He was either with Aimee or Jaxson. To make sure my familiar wasn't in any trouble, I called my boyfriend.

"Hey, there, where have you been? I thought you would

have called a while ago," he said.

"I was only gone two hours. I have a lot of news. We can talk about it over dinner."

"Sounds wonderful."

"Let me clean up, and I'll be right over."

"Perfect."

"Is Iggy with you?" I asked.

"You bet."

Good. That was one less thing I had to worry about. I rushed into the bathroom, taking off my clothes as I went. After a quick shower, I threw on a pair of jeans and a cute pink top. With my large purse in hand, I walked to the office.

As soon as I stepped inside, I looked around for my familiar. "Where's Iggy?"

He crawled out from under the sofa. "Just hanging out. Jaxson said you had news?"

"I do. You can come with us to dinner if you like."

"You only want me to come with you, so you won't have to repeat stuff."

My iguana knew me so well. "That's only partially true. I've missed you."

"Whatever," Iggy said as he waddled toward me.

His attitude really needed adjusting.

Jaxson grabbed his wallet and keys while I picked up Iggy. As we were halfway to the door, a man appeared in our main room—and by appear, I mean he just materialized in front of us.

# Chapter Five

I HAD TO be imagining this. People didn't just appear out of thin air. I blinked three times to make sure what I was seeing was real. *Wait a minute*. "Dominic Geno? Is that you?"

This man was someone we'd met in Ohio this past Christmas—in the year 1972. He was wearing a suit that wasn't exactly in style, but he appeared solid enough—not like the usual ghosts I'd encountered in the past.

His mouth was hanging open, and his gaze was bouncing all around the room. "Where am I?" he whispered.

At least we were both confused. I looked over at Jaxson, hoping he was seeing what I was. I'm not sure what I'd do if this vision was a figment of my imagination. Take a vacation to get my head on straight, I suppose.

Without thinking, I reached out and touched his chest. Yup. He was solid all right. "I'm sorry. I wanted to be sure you were real."

"I'm real, or maybe I'm dreaming."

"I don't think you are." Jaxson moved closer. "Do you know who *we* are?"

Thank goodness Jaxson saw him, which meant I wasn't crazy.

Dominic closed his mouth. "Of course. You're Jaxson

from Witch's Cove." He looked over at me. "And you're Glinda."

Relief poured through me.

"What about me?" Iggy asked.

I looked down at my familiar. "Iggy, Mr. Geno can't understand you. He's not a warlock."

"I heard him. Or rather I heard someone." He looked between Jaxson and me. "Is one of you a ventriloquist?" Dominic stabbed his fingers through his hair. I swear he'd aged five years in the last few seconds alone. The poor man seemed about to fall apart.

"No. My animal can talk, but it's a long story." I'd address the issue of Dominic being a warlock later. A person could only take in so much at once.

"Tell me what is going on," he said. "Nothing is making sense. One minute I'm in Ohio, and the next I'm here."

While we had planned to go out to dinner, we had to deal with Dominic right now. "I think I might know. Kind of. Sort of."

Jaxson motioned Dom take a seat on the sofa. "Thanks," our new visitor said.

"Can I get you a coffee, maybe?" I asked.

He blew out a breath. "That would be great."

He probably would have preferred something stronger, but we didn't have any liquor in our office. I placed Iggy on the table in front of Dominic and then went into our makeshift kitchen. Could our time traveler really hear Iggy? When we had been in Ohio where we'd met Dom, he couldn't—or at least he never said he could—understand my familiar. And here I thought finding a skeleton in a wall had been the strangest thing I'd had to deal with this week.

I fixed us some drinks and picked up a few leaves for Iggy to munch on. All I had in the way of snacks were some crackers and cheese, which I placed on a tray and then carried them out.

I set everything down and then scooted next to Jaxson.

"Jaxson just told me this is the twenty-first century," Dominic said. "Is that true?"

"Yes." I held up my phone and asked Siri what the year was. When her voice—which probably sounded strange to Dominic—told us the day and year, he once more appeared dumbfounded—and I couldn't blame him. I remember how disoriented I had been when we found ourselves in snowy Ohio after having walked down the street in balmy Witch's Cove only seconds before.

"How is that possible? And how did that person talk from inside that thing? I mean, I understand television and all, but that makes no sense."

Oh, boy. "This is a cell phone. It's really just a portable landline, but we have other things to deal with besides how technology works." That might not have come across as very sympathetic, but I couldn't help him until I understood how he ended up here.

After blowing on his coffee, Dominic drank the still hot brew. "Am I crazy or did I just meet you two, or rather the four of you, at Christmas in Charlotte in 1972."

After we'd figured out who had murdered Michael Hamstead, it had been Dominic who dropped the bomb that he was an undercover FBI agent and not some graduate student as he'd claimed. Now we had to tell him about time travel.

"Yes, but it's a really long story."

He looked around. "Where is your niece? What was her name?"

"Rihanna is my cousin. She is out with her boyfriend, but she should be back shortly."

He held onto his mug as if it was his lifeline to his sanity. "I'm not sure I can grasp all of this."

Jaxson slapped his thighs. "How about I order some take out?" He turned to me. "What we are about to tell Dominic probably shouldn't be talked about in public."

My partner was always thinking. "Good idea."

He turned to our bewildered time traveler. "Do you like pizza?"

"Who doesn't?"

"Great." Jaxson pulled out his cell and placed the order. The whole time Dominic stared at Jaxson, his brows were pinched in concentration. When Jaxson hung up, Dominic sucked in a big breath. "I'm still not believing someone can make a phone call on something that small."

Everything would be new to him. At least when Jaxson, Rihanna, Iggy, and I went back in time, we had no big surprises, other than dealing with no personal computers, no cell phones, and bad television reception. For the most part, it was business as usual. Okay, the lack of Uber had been a downer, but we'd managed. But for Dominic, time traveling forward would be quite the shock. The future could be a scary place.

"Yes, and I'm sure there are a lot more surprises to come." I looked over at Jaxson. "Do you want to start?"

He pointed a finger at me. "Be my guest."

Great. I turned back to Dominic, not sure how to explain something that even I didn't fully understand. "Basically, you time traveled about fifty years into the future."

"Jaxson claimed that, and I want to say that concept doesn't exist, yet here I am." His brows pinched. "Or are you guys tech geniuses who have all this advanced stuff?"

"Nothing advanced in this room. No, pretty much everyone has computers and cell phones." We might have to talk about solar panels, self-driving cars, microwaves, and smart televisions at one point. Just not now.

"This is insane."

"Insane or not, for whatever reason, you're here now."

He blew out a breath. "So it seems. My buddies back home are not going to believe it."

"Few will." I guess I was lucky that many of the gossip queens accepted my story right away and had been willing to help me get Jaxson, Rihanna, and Iggy back.

"Considering the way you both are dressed, along with your electronic devices, we are not in my time, but how do I know you didn't kidnap me and stage it to make it look like the future?" he asked.

Poor Dominic was trying to make sense of all of this, and I couldn't blame him. "How about we walk outside to the parking lot? You'll see all of the cars are quite different, too, and maybe other things."

"I'd like to see that."

It might also show him we hadn't kidnapped him. The three of us went outside. It was almost fun to see Dominic run his hand over several of the car hoods. "They are rather small, aren't they?"

"Definitely, which makes them more efficient."

"I like that."

Cars buzzed by on the street. He studied the street lights and the buildings across the road, mouthing the word *wow* many times. I bet it would be fun to see the future through his eyes.

"Are you convinced we didn't drug you and try to fool you into thinking this is the future? Don't worry, there is a lot more we can show you." The high definition television would blow his mind.

"Yes, but it's going to take me some time to process all of this."

"We understand. Come back inside," Jaxson said. "The food will be here soon."

Once we were all seated, I turned to Dominic. "It might help if you told us what you were doing right before you appeared here." Had he located a gold coin like the one we had found?

"Sure, I was back in Charlotte, Ohio with Stephanie Carlton. You remember her, right?'

"Yes."

"Well, we were there to testify in the murder trial of Michael Hamstead."

"Were you in the courtroom when you transported here?" Jaxson asked.

"No, actually we'd finished our testimony. I had gone back to the hotel, preparing to fly back to Washington the next day. That's where I live."

That made no sense. He didn't do anything to trigger the spell—if that was what it was called? "By any chance did you talk to Bethany Criant when you were in Charlotte?"

"Not on this trip. Why?"

"No reason."

"Tell him, Glinda," Jaxson said.

"Okay, I thought she might have given you something of magic, like a gold coin. That's what enabled us to time travel back and forth."

"I never saw a coin." He stuck his hand in his pocket, pulled out a pink ribbon, and handed it to me. "Only this. Please don't judge, but this might belong to you."

My pulse shot up. "I can't believe it. Yes, or at least I think it's mine. I had wrapped it around some mistletoe that my iguana here had partially eaten."

Iggy looked off to the side. "Hold a grudge much?"

"Not anymore." Sheesh.

Dominic leaned forward. "The ribbon had come off the sprig of mistletoe, so I picked it up."

"That was months ago," I said.

"I meant, I found it right after you left. I spotted the mistletoe in the hallway of the B&B. As corny as it might sound, to me, this ribbon represented hope that someday I'd find someone to love."

Aw. That was so romantic.

The timing worked then. Someone knocked on our door, and Jaxson jumped up. "That was fast," he said.

After paying the pizza delivery person, Jaxson carried in the food and set it on the coffee table.

Dominic smiled. "Now, this reminds me of home."

"I don't think pizza has changed over the years. Dig in."

For the next few minutes we ate, enjoying every bite—or

at least I did.

"Maybe I should keep the pink ribbon," Dominic said. "That is, if you think I could use it to get back to my time."

"Of course." I handed it back to him. "I have no idea if that was what did it. I honestly thought that when I kissed Jaxson under the mistletoe that it contained magic. In the end, it was a coin that Bethany Criant had put in my possession that did it."

"I saw no gold coin anywhere." For a moment, he closed his eyes. When he opened them again, he let out a breath. "It didn't work. You both time traveled. How did you do it again?"

"Like I said, I'm pretty sure it was the gold coin that I believe Madam Criant gave us."

"The psychic was for real?" he asked.

"Yes. Turns out she was the college roommate of one of our most powerful witches here in Witch's Cove—a Gertrude Poole."

His eyes darted back and forth. "That would make her…old."

"She's almost ninety, but she's quite spry."

"Can we ask her to help?" he asked.

"Sure, but we'll have to wait until tomorrow. Even then, there is no guarantee she can help you." I explained how she would have to contact Bethany Criant in the spirit world for information, since Madam Criant had passed away over two years ago. I turned to Jaxson. "You said the gold coin just appeared in front of Iggy after I'd returned back to our time?"

"Yes."

I faced Dominic. "Maybe, you'll get lucky, and one will

show up for you."

The front door opened, and Rihanna breezed in. She'd taken two steps before she stopped. "Dominic Geno?" She stared at him, no doubt trying to figure out what was going on.

Iggy did a circle. "Isn't this fun? He came from the past."

"I guess so." She turned to me. "You should have called me. I would have come back right away."

"Rihanna, I just got here," Dominic said. "Or rather, I more or less just appeared here, walked around a bit, and ate some pizza."

Her gaze went from his head to his wing tipped shoes. "You might need a wardrobe change if you plan on staying."

I had to laugh. "Sorry, but it's true."

Rihanna sat down. "How did you end up in Glinda and Jaxson's office?" she asked.

He dipped in his chin. "You tell me that, and it will be a bigger story than Kennedy's assassination."

Wait until he learned about the destruction of the World Trade Center, though the concept of time travel would rock the world more than that if it became public knowledge. I wonder how many people would want to go back—or forward in time? Would I want to know what was in store for me and Jaxson? It took all of about ten seconds to decide. No, I would not. If I saw that the future was amazing, I'd rush to get there and ruin it somehow.

Jaxson looked over at Dominic. "I have a spare bedroom at my apartment. How about you crash there until we can figure out how to get you back to your time?"

"That would be fantastic." He patted his pockets, pulled

out his wallet, and opened it. "Do they still take dollars here?"

We laughed. "Yes, some things haven't changed, but most pay by credit card." He would learn that his dollar didn't go nearly as far as it did fifty years ago.

He waved his credit card. "Do you think Washington Mutual still exists?"

"Let me check." Jaxson stood and went over to his computer.

Dominic's eyes sparkled. "Go ahead and watch, Dominic. You will be blown away," I said.

"Thanks." He sat next to Jaxson, saying nothing as a list of names appeared on the screen. "You have to be kidding me. Hundreds of banks have failed?"

"Afraid so," Jaxson said.

If Dominic was forced to stay here, he might have to get an economics lesson, and I didn't envy him one bit.

# Chapter Six

THE NEXT MORNING, I arrived at the office before Jaxson, which was a rarity. If I had to guess, he was teaching Dominic the ways of the modern world.

As I set down my purse, Rihanna walked out of her bedroom with her arms outstretched in a welcoming pose. "You're here early."

"I couldn't really sleep."

She smiled and then sighed. "I guess it's not every day a time traveler lands in our office."

"No." We'd talked a bit last night after Jaxson and Dominic left. "Did you come up with any ideas on how to send him back?" I asked.

"I'm thinking we should do a séance with Madam Criant. She sent us back in time. Most likely she is responsible for sending Dominic here."

"I was thinking the same thing. Any thoughts as to why she'd want him in our time? From what Dominic told us, those two weren't close. In fact, he didn't even see her when he returned to Charlotte for the trial."

Rihanna's eyes widened, as if something just occurred to her. "It is a coincidence that you found a fifty-year-old skeleton right when an FBI agent comes here from fifty years in the past?"

Oh, my goodness. "How did I not see that? That has to be it. Do you think Madam Criant believes that Dominic killed this man and wants him to pay? Could this dead man be her new husband, Evan Drugan, by any chance?" I don't know why I picked Evan, since I had no idea if the man was even dead, but he was the first name that came to mind.

My cousin huffed. "I don't think FBI agents go around killing cooks."

"Who's to say he wasn't some criminal who had a penchant for cooking? The problem is that I really didn't know much about Madam Criant's husband." I snapped my fingers. "Let's look on the Internet. If Evan Drugan was murdered fifty years ago, the information should be someplace."

She flashed me a smile. "I'll grab my computer, and we can both search."

"Good idea." She was better with technology than I was.

"Call Jaxson," Iggy said. "He'll do it faster and better."

While true, it hurt that my familiar was so fickle—one minute thinking I was the best and the next claiming that no one could beat Jaxson Harrison. I should be happy that Iggy adored the man I loved, but my ego could use a bit of stroking every now and again.

"I will contact Jaxson, but let me check it out first. I'm not bad using a computer, you know." It would be a problem if we ended up tipping off Dominic that we thought he'd killed the man, should he be responsible for his death.

Iggy hopped up next to me. "Show me. What do ya got?"

"Smarty pants." I typed in Evan's name, along with the name of the town. It took a few tries before I found where he'd lived and when he died. "I got it," I called to my cousin.

She came out carrying her computer. "I found some interesting stuff, too, but you go first."

"Our skeleton is not Evan Drugan since he only passed away ten years ago."

"Oh."

"You?"

She inhaled. "I figured we'd be more productive if I checked out Dominic Geno, FBI agent. It took a bit of work, but I found he went missing in 1973."

I whistled. "He really did teleport to our time. It doesn't say if he is dead, does it?"

"Nope, just that he is suspected to be dead, possibly killed by the man he was hunting."

My pulse sped up. "Who was the man?"

"His name was Raymond Gonzalez." She scanned the page. "The man was quite evil, leaving several bodies in his path from Virginia to Ohio."

"Do you think Dominic killed him instead, and the man in the wall is this guy?"

My cousin laughed. "Seriously? When Dominic gets here, we'll ask him if he's ever been to Witch's Cove before. I think he would have mentioned it if he had been."

"True." As if we had summoned him, the office door opened, and Jaxson and Dominic came in.

Iggy made some strange noise that I bet he thought was a whistle—only he failed. "You look a lot better," my familiar said.

That implied Dominic looked bad in his suit yesterday. "Iggy."

"What? His clothes were funny looking. Even Rihanna thought so."

Dominic held up a hand. "My clothes, young man, were very stylish back in the seventies."

I didn't recognize what he was wearing. They weren't Jaxson's clothes. "Where did you go shopping?"

"We didn't," Jaxson said. "You won't believe it. When we got back to my house, what should we find on the spare bed but a suitcase."

That was exactly what happened when we all teleported back in time to Ohio. "Don't tell me the clothes were his size?"

"Yup," Dominic said. "Right down to the shoes."

"Then it has to be Bethany Criant who is behind this."

"The psychic lady?" Dominic asked.

"Yes."

"Was there a driver's license and stuff, like there had been for us?" Rihanna asked.

Jaxson nodded to Dominic, who pulled out his wallet. "Yes. The scary part is that whoever is doing this almost wants me to stay."

"Why is that?" I asked.

"I have a Florida driver's license with Jaxson's address on it. My birthday is listed as 1987 instead of 1937."

"That's what happened to us. I'd show you our licenses, but when we teleported back here, nothing from back then came with us—not even our 70's clothes."

"There's more," Jaxson said. "Show them, Dom."

Dominic pulled out a social security card and a health card. "It's like I really am from this time, but you know I'm not, right?"

"Yes, we know you're not."

He stuffed his wallet back into his pocket. "Do you have any coffee or know where I can get some? I can't think straight without it, and I really need to be on my game."

I looked over at Jaxson. "How about we go to the Tiki Hut?"

"Didn't you tell me Penny was working this morning?" he asked.

"Yes, but I'll tell her not to say anything." I turned to Dominic. "My aunt owns the Tiki Hut Grill, but she knows we time traveled back to your time. She will keep quiet if I ask her to." Or so I hoped.

"Sounds good. I'll try to keep my comments neutral."

As an FBI agent, I bet he could pull it off. "Then let's go."

"I'm coming," Iggy said.

"Fine. You can help Aunt Fern."

He tilted his head. "You're no fun. I want to be in the middle of the action."

I smiled. "I promise to fill you in on everything when we finish."

"Be that way. See if I help you solve this case." Iggy turned his eyes away from me. It was his passive aggressive pose.

I laughed. "Come on."

Iggy knew the routine. He crawled into my purse, and off we went. During the short walk to the restaurant, Dominic's head swiveled, seeming to enjoy what the future might bring. Witch's Cove was a small beach town that hadn't changed much since I was born. For Dominic, that might be an easier pill to swallow.

Before we reached the restaurant, I looked over at him. "Have you ever been to Witch's Cove before?"

"Nope. Never."

"You don't know what you're missing," my lie-detecting cousin said. That was her way of letting me know that to his knowledge, he was telling the truth.

If that was the case, then the skeleton in the wall wasn't the man who Dominic had been chasing. I'd bring up Raymond Gonzalez and his alleged crimes when we weren't in a public place.

I figured we'd have breakfast, and then see if Gertrude could help us contact her good friend Bethany Criant from the hereafter.

As soon as I walked into the restaurant, my aunt rushed over. "Table for four?" Her brows rose.

"Aunt Fern, this is Dominic Geno who helped with the case in Charlotte, Ohio when we visited over Christmas."

Her brows pinched. "I'm not sure I understand."

I leaned forward. "He time traveled here last night, but don't say a word. And I'm serious!"

She leaned back. "I wouldn't dare. No one would believe me anyway, other than my friends. After all, they helped bring Jaxson, Rihanna, and Iggy back from the past."

"I know." We had tried to contact Bethany back then, too. "Please know that if it got out that Dom was from back then, he'd be pestered to death. Just so you know, he will deny it, and people will think you're the crazy one."

I looked over at him, and he smiled sweetly at my aunt. "If Glinda thinks it is for the best, I will keep quiet also," he said. "Just so you know, I have a driver's license to prove that I was born thirty-five years ago, not eighty-five years ago, which was the case."

My aunt lifted her chin. "Fine, but I want to be kept in the loop."

I hugged her. "I promise. Now can we get a table?"

She grinned. "Of course. You can take table two. It's in Penny's section."

"Thank you." I handed her Iggy.

My aunt instantly smiled and cooed at him. "You haven't visited me in a while."

"Sorry. I've been preoccupied."

"That's okay. We can chat now."

My poor Aunt. Ever since Uncle Harold's ghost passed over permanently, she'd been lonely. Sure, she'd had a few boyfriends, but they either ended up being creeps or dying.

As soon as we were seated, my best friend rushed over. Even though she was still dating her hot forest ranger, Penny would be interested in the identity of the newcomer. At least, she knew all about my time-traveling adventure, so I wouldn't have to keep anything from her.

"Hi, everyone." She looked over at Dominic, obviously wanting an introduction.

"Penny, this is Dominic Geno. He's an FBI agent."

"Ooh. Are you here about the skeleton? Do you know who it is yet?"

Whoa. "No! We met him at *Christmas*. I was as surprised as anyone that he just showed up on our doorstep last night." I pressed my lips together and raised my brows to indicate she shouldn't ask any more questions.

"Oh, you're *that* FBI agent. How long are you staying, Dominic?"

"I don't know."

She cleared her throat. Thankfully, she seemed to understand the delicacy of the situation. "Do you know what you'd like?"

"For starters, we'd all like coffee," I said.

"Gotcha." She winked and hurried to the coffee station.

Dominic leaned forward. "What's this about a skeleton?"

I had hoped that Rihanna could tell if he truly was in the dark about the body. "It was so strange." I explained about how I was talking with the new owner, Courtney Higgins, when the workers doing the renovation on the fifty-year-old building uncovered a skeleton tucked away in the wall.

"You don't know who it is, I take it?"

"No, but the man was about forty-five. The medical examiner is sending the skull off for some 3-D scan so we can get a clay model likeness, and the bones will undergo carbon-14 testing to determine when the person died."

"What's a 3-D scan?" he asked.

I kept forgetting this technology and much of what we discussed wouldn't have been around in his time. "Jaxson, would you do the honors of explaining it?"

He smiled. "Sure." He actually gave an explanation I could understand, but the idea of digital scans was kind of lost on Dominic, even though he seemed very excited to learn more.

I was hoping Dominic might have offered a suggestion as to the man's identity—such as the skeleton could have been that serial killer wanted by the FBI—but he didn't seem to have any connection to this man. So, why was Dominic here?

When we'd been sent back in time, I was told it was so that Bethany Criant, Gertrude Poole's college roommate, could meet us. I thought that was a bit excessive, but who knows? Maybe she just wanted to know more about the future. If she had conversed with Gertrude later on, we never learned about it.

Penny returned with our drinks. While we ordered, Dominic looked over the rather extensive menu. I wanted to help him out. "Try the cheese omelet with mushrooms. It's divine."

He smiled. "Perfect." He looked up at Penny. "I'll have that."

"You got it."

No sooner had she left than Courtney came in. That was a nice surprise. She looked around, probably to see how crowded it was. When she spotted us, she stopped in her tracks, her gaze focused solely on Dominic.

I won't lie. The man is good looking, but was he worth the shocked look on her face? Maybe not, but that was because I had Jaxson. Since I understood how uncomfortable it was to eat alone, I raised my hand and motioned for Courtney to join us.

She seemed to break out of her trance. With a smile, she walked toward us. "Glinda! I didn't expect to see you here."

I don't know why I wouldn't be here. She knew my aunt owned the place. "Would you care to sit with us?"

"I'd love to."

Being a gentleman, Dominic grabbed a chair from another table and placed it next to him. "Sit by me. I'm a newcomer."

"Oh, really?"

This breakfast suddenly took a more interesting turn.

Dominic stuck out his hand and told her his name and that he was here from Virginia. Since Courtney had not met Rihanna or Jaxson, I made the introductions. Iggy crawled over, no doubt unable to stay out of the limelight. I was thankful he was adept at avoiding any customers walking by.

My familiar crawled up my leg and onto the table, which I thought was a bit forward. For one, Courtney hadn't met my familiar yet.

"Hi, I'm Iggy," he said to her.

Her eyes widened. "You can talk?"

Oh, boy, that just made things even more bizarre. Did our two newcomers both have some form of magical powers? It was always possible someone had put a spell on them, giving them the ability to converse with familiars, but it was also possible they had innate talents. The question was did they know it? Courtney never told me she was a witch, even though I confessed I was one. The surprises kept coming.

# Chapter Seven

"COURTNEY IS REMODELING the burned out bookstore across the street, which is where the skeleton was found," I said as a way of explaining exactly who she was.

"You didn't have to tell him about that." Courtney might have been smiling, but her tone implied she was not happy with me.

"Don't worry. Dominic is an FBI agent. I thought he might know something about the body." So what if he said he didn't have a clue.

"Do you?" Courtney asked with renewed hope. "I'd loved to get the mystery solved so people will stop being scared of what was in the wall."

I wasn't sure how knowing the man's identity would prevent anyone from being creeped out by it, but I said nothing for a change.

"I don't have any idea, yet, but maybe you can show me where you found the body. Perhaps I can help," Dominic said.

I loved when a plan came together. They both were looking for love. Why not help that along?

She grinned. "I'd like that."

As if they were the only two at the table, they chatted about her store. I was impressed that Dominic was incredibly adept at not directly answering any of the questions that would indicate he was from another time.

Courtney pulled out her phone. "How about we exchange numbers?"

Oh, no. Dominic didn't own a phone.

"Ah, Dominic left his phone at the apartment, but tell me, and I'll put your cell number in mine," Jaxson said.

That was smart. Clearly, we'd have to fix Dominic up with a spare phone or chance him being found out, something that would cause many questions to arise.

Once they exchanged contact information, we finished eating. Courtney then excused herself, saying she had to get back to the shop. "Once you are settled, call me," she told Dominic with a smile. "I'd love to show you the store and where *he* was found."

"I will." I was thrilled at how his eyes sparkled. Dominic watched her until she was out the door. Only then did he turn back to us. "I didn't expect that."

"Expect what?"

"To meet someone on my first full day into the future."

I smiled. "She seems interested."

"I had that sense, too, but I'll slip up eventually. What will happen if she learns I'm from the past?"

That was the big question. "She'll either be eternally curious and not leave you alone, or she'll avoid you."

Rihanna, who hadn't said much, shook her head. "Courtney seems really level-headed. I think she'd be okay with it, assuming she believes you."

"I don't plan to come out and make an announcement, but if she asks me to do something, such as turn on a computer, I'd have a hard time explaining how I was an ignorant FBI agent."

He had a point. "Let's take it one step at a time. Right now, we need to see if Gertrude knows how you got here, why you are here, and how to return you to your time."

Dominic chuckled. "I'd love to find out, but I have to say, after today, I might not be in a real hurry to get back."

Whoa. Maybe going into the future was more fun than I'd thought. For me, it would largely depend on who I was leaving behind. "There's a lot to be said for the twenty-first century."

"So it seems."

After I gathered up Iggy and paid, we all headed to the Psychics Corner.

On the way, I called to make an appointment but then asked the secretary to let me speak with Gertrude directly. I wanted to give her a heads up as to who Dominic Geno was. Thankfully, she remembered the whole time travel event that had occurred months before. After I hung up, I told them that Gertrude would be happy to see us.

Once we stepped inside her office, the psychic stood, came over to Dominic, and clasped his hands. She then closed her eyes and inhaled. He looked over at us and mouthed, "What is she doing?"

Gertrude smiled. "I'm trying to see if I can hear Bethany. If she sent you, she would have transferred a message."

When Dominic jerked his hands out of her grasp, Rihanna laughed. "Sorry. We should have warned you about Gertrude's abilities. I keep forgetting how creepy it can be when someone reads your mind."

He looked between us. "Can she really read minds?"

We all nodded. Gertrude smiled. "Let's sit down. I think Dominic here needs to rest."

I felt a little sorry for him. He kept being bombarded with one shock after another.

"I need to know what happened, Dominic," Gertrude said. "Start with what you were doing before you arrived here." She chuckled. "Arriving here makes it sound as if you came on a plane, but you know what I mean."

He repeated what he told us, including finding the pink ribbon. "I'm embarrassed to say I was hoping there was a little bit of magic in the material. I saw how Glinda and Jaxson looked at each other."

"That trip was special," I said, wanting to confirm that I thought the same thing.

"When did you last speak with Bethany Criant," Gertrude asked, ignoring the idea that the ribbon might hold some special love power.

"I saw her at Christmas dinner held at the B&B. Since she wasn't staying there, and we had caught Michael Hamstead's killer, I never followed up with her."

"I see." Gertrude turned to me. "Did you mention Dominic's name to Bethany after that?"

I had to think about it. "I really can't remember. I didn't even know he was an FBI agent until right before I returned to the present."

Jaxson glanced at Rihanna. "We stayed for about five more days and talked to Madam Criant upon her return from her honeymoon since we were desperate to come back to our time," Jaxson said. "We told her quite a lot about what had transpired, though I'm not sure what I could have told her other than Dominic wasn't who he claimed to be."

"Perhaps we should ask her. Would anyone like to try to contact Bethany?" Gertrude said.

"Yes." All of us but Dominic answered, probably because he wasn't sure what that entailed. Or maybe he was unaware that she had passed.

Gertrude turned to him. "Don't worry. She won't reveal any deep, dark secrets of yours." Wow. She had tapped into his thoughts.

"Good to know," he said.

"Great. Boys, help drag the table to the center. Jaxson, you know the drill."

He and Dominic carried the table to the middle of the room while Rihanna located the candles. Gertrude instructed where everyone should sit and how to keep our fingers connected at all times. Iggy crawled between me and Rihanna, his usual spot for séances.

"I don't know if Bethany will contact us. The longer she's been gone, the weaker the signal," Gertrude said.

I didn't know that. Our psychic might have said that in case Bethany didn't want to contact anyone today. Disappointing Dominic might affect his psyche.

Once we closed our eyes, Gertrude began. "Bethany Criant, I call upon you today because a young traveler, Dominic Geno, is with us. Did you send him to us? And if so, why?"

I understood that it often took time for the spirit to either appear as a ghost, speak through someone, or talk to the person. Since Gertrude was Bethany's good friend, any one of the above options was a possibility.

"No. I can't," Gertrude blurted thirty seconds later. "You didn't? Who did?…How can he get back?"

I could guess what the second part meant but not the first. I behaved myself and didn't move my hands or open my eyes. Iggy wouldn't have as much control. If he spotted a ghost, he'd let me know.

"Bethany? Don't go!" The slight panic in Gertrude's voice almost scared me. "Oh, no, she's gone," she said, her voice fading away.

Even though my eyes were closed, I could tell the lit candles had gone out. Whether Gertrude had blown them out or Bethany's spirit had done it, I couldn't say.

I opened my eyes and pretended to relax back in my chair. "What did she say?"

Gertrude shook her head. "She didn't send Dominic, but she sensed it might have been someone close to her."

"So she has no idea why he is here?" I asked.

"No."

That didn't help. "Did she say how he can get back?"

"Kind of. Someone will send a sign."

A sign? "What does that mean?"

"I don't know. I'm sorry. It's all she told me. If you all would excuse me, I need to rest." She pushed back her chair.

What? Gertrude never said she needed to rest after a séance. Something funky was going on, but I hoped she'd see fit to tell us when she was ready. "Thank you for contacting Bethany. I guess we just have to wait."

"Yes. You need to wait."

I didn't like that answer, but we didn't have much choice.

After we made sure Gertrude was okay, we left. Jaxson paid on the way out as I was a bit upset with what happened. I really had hoped for a solution to Dominic's dilemma.

"Let's go back to the office," I said. "We need to make a plan."

Jaxson turned to Dominic. "That's Glinda's way of getting some control over what happened."

"That's not a bad thing, you know," I shot back.

Jaxson wrapped an arm around my shoulder and then kissed the top of my head. "No, it's not."

When we were settled into the office, Rihanna plopped down. "Something was bothering Gertrude."

"Do you have any idea what?"

"I felt a flash of fear and then anger."

"About?" I asked.

"I don't know since she instantly blocked me. Gertrude is powerful enough to prevent anyone from hearing her thoughts."

That didn't surprise me. "Are we to go about our business as usual until a sign appears that allows Dominic to return to his past?" I looked over at my cousin since she seemed to have a connection to Gertrude.

"That would be my guess."

Frustration welled. "We have to wait for the skeleton's face to be created, we have to wait to find out when he died, and we have to wait for some unknown sign in order to help Dominic return." I turned to our newcomer. "I'm really bad at waiting."

"There has to be a silver lining to all of this somewhere." Dominic turned to Jaxson. "If the offer still stands, I'd like to learn my way around Witch's Cove and get a crash course in computers, cell phones, and that fast cooking microwave."

Jaxson smiled. "My pleasure. I have an old cell phone I don't use anymore. We can get you set up with a phone plan. Once you have a number, you will be good to go."

"You all are so generous. I'd like to pay you back somehow. If you need anyone to do surveillance, I'm your man. Thankfully, driving doesn't seem to have changed much over the years." He held up his hand. "Jaxson did have to show me how to pump gas this morning and how to use the credit card in the machine, but other than that, it seemed the same."

He was so calm, unlike me. "What will happen if we don't get any sign that shows you the way home?" I asked.

Dominic's brows rose. "Then I won't have a choice but to stay here. If that happens, once I acclimate to this new world, I would like to find a job."

What a great attitude. "That sounds like a good solution."

Rihanna stood. "I'm going to check on Gavin. He might know something or at least know the status of the skeleton."

"That would be great."

"And I am going to check on Courtney and the location of the mystery man. I doubt I can help, but who knows?" Dominic said.

He wanted to spend time with her, and I couldn't blame him. "I'm sure she'll be happy to see you."

Once Rihanna and Dominic left, I leaned against Jaxson. "Now what?"

"We should come up with a list of things we want to do when we have no cases on the docket," he said.

"What do you suggest?"

"We could take a walk on the beach, go to the movies, read a book, or even take up knitting."

I punched him. "You would never knit. Actually, I don't see myself knitting either. Now, if you were busy, I suppose I could bother Levy and his coven about reading up on spells and such. His library is vast."

"I like it. I'm sure I'll be spending some time with Dominic, unless he volunteers to help Courtney in her store. She might even decide to teach him about the ways of the world."

I smiled. "That would make the time pass quickly for him." I looked up at Jaxson. "Uh-oh. forgot. I need to call Andorra."

"What for?"

I explained that Elissa thought Andorra might be able to provide more information about the cause of the skeleton's death.

"Other than magic?"

"Sort of. I believe Andorra will say it's magic, but perhaps she can be more specific. I honestly don't know the extent of her talents."

"Call her," he said.

She answered on the second ring. "Glinda, I've been meaning to get back to you."

"About the skeleton?"

"Yes. I was delighted that Dr. Sanchez asked for my help."

I was happy, too. "Did you learn anything?"

"You were right that magic killed him, but I sensed this person of magic used a spell based on a potion that contained some of the ingredients we sell at the store. Mind you, there are stores in neighboring towns that sell the same things, so it doesn't necessarily narrow it down to Witch's Cove."

"Would your grandmother know anything about this spell?" I didn't think Hex and Bones existed fifty years ago, though. "I thought she only opened the store in the last twenty years."

"You have a good memory, but Memaw had a small shop on the edge of town a long time ago. I don't know if she sold those particular herbs back then, but the man definitely died from a spell. The exact nature of it, I couldn't say."

I wasn't sure how much that would help us figure out his identity, but it was better than what I had learned. "That might come in useful."

"I hope so."

"The four of us need to get together real soon." Even though we hadn't had any clients in the last two weeks, either Drake or Andorra had been busy.

"Totally. Look, I have to go. Some customers just came in."

"Go, take care of them."

"Later."

I disconnected and sighed. "I could use that walk on the beach right about now. I'll tell you everything."

"I love it."

"I am not coming if you guys kiss," Iggy said.

We both laughed. "Then I guess you'll have to stay here, buddy."

# Chapter Eight

THE NEXT TWO weeks were really hard—or at least for me they were—because no one stopped by our office to ask for our help, which was a little disheartening. At least it prompted me to come up with a better marketing plan. Unfortunately, it hadn't started to work yet.

On a slightly more positive note, I heard back from Dahlia who had researched all of missing persons' cases in Witch's Cove from a long time ago. Like Sheriff Rocker, she'd come up empty-handed.

When Jaxson had some spare time, he searched for some information on the identity of our skeleton, but so far, he'd hit one dead end after another. In all fairness, his time had been limited, because he was often giving Dominic lessons on technology.

In between the welcome-to-the-future classes, Jaxson researched some old FBI cases, hoping one would shed some light on this mystery man. Dominic had given Jaxson a list of the cases he'd been involved in, but I didn't see how that would help us figure out anything now.

I was sitting on the office sofa reading a fairly boring book when my cell rang. "It's Elissa," I told Jaxson who was hunched over the computer. Finally, some action—or so I hope.

"Elissa, nice to hear from you. I've been sitting on pins and needles. Tell me you know something."

"I've been as anxious as you to learn about this skeleton, and I finally have a clue. I'm going to send you a photo of the finished image of the face. I asked Nash and Steve to scan their databases for a hit, but unless the old files have been digitized, electronic copies of criminals weren't around fifty years ago, so I'm not holding my breath that they will come up with anything."

The timing wasn't lost on me. If Dominic came from fifty years ago, he might know this man. So what if he'd never been to Witch's Cove. "Thank you so much. Someone has to know his identity. Were they able to figure out where he's from?"

She chuckled. "We've advanced over the years but not far enough in my opinion. Our best hope is that his shoes will give us a clue. The lab in Tampa is still working on that and the rest of his clothing."

"Thanks for letting me know. If you learn anything else, call me."

"Will do." As soon as I disconnected, my phone chimed, indicating she'd sent the picture of the clay model of the man's face.

I opened it and then walked over to where Jaxson was sitting. "Here is our guy." I showed him the face.

"They got the hair length right, but I will never understand how they can figure out ear and nose shape."

"I agree."

"Let me text Dominic to let him know we have the man's image. I just hope he remembers to check his messages now and again."

"It would be too good to be true if he recognizes him."

"Wouldn't it though?" Jaxson said.

"Dominic mentioned he was planning to spend the day with Courtney. We could stretch our legs and walk over to the candy store. In fact, I'd like to see the progress of the shop. I heard Courtney is about to open."

"I say we go."

I didn't see Iggy, so the two of us took off. When we entered the candy store, Courtney and Dominic were in the main room filling the finished shelves with colorful candy. According to Dominic, the back room—the one that used to house her desk and makeshift kitchen—was in the process of being remodeled.

"Hey, guys," I said. "We just came to check out the progress of the store. It looks amazing." My mouth dropped open when I saw the fountain bar on the side. "You took my suggestion!"

"Yes. I want people to be able to hang out and enjoy themselves."

And eat lots of candy. "I can't wait. When do you think you'll open?" The kids were out for summer vacation, so now would be a great time.

"Soon. The workers are dismantling the back room, and they said it would take about a week to rebuild it all."

"That is so exciting." I pointed to the skeleton sticking out of the wall, along with the witch's caldron right below it. "I love the new décor."

"It is fun, isn't it?"

I turned to Dominic. "Can we talk to you for a moment

outside?" I raised my brows.

"Sure, but I have nothing to hide from Courtney."

What did that mean? Had he told her he was a time traveler? I hope so, or this discussion could become awkward fast. I pulled out my phone. "Do you recognize this man?"

Dominic studied the image for all of three seconds. "That's Raymond Gonzalez. He's the man I've been searching for. He's on the FBI's most wanted list. Where did you get this?"

I stepped closer so I could keep my voice low. "He's the skeleton."

His face paled. "But how?"

Did he suddenly forget that fifty years had passed? "I don't know. He must have traveled to Witch's Cove and met his death."

Courtney stepped next to him. "What's wrong? You look like you've seen a ghost, Dom."

"Maybe I have."

I still wasn't sure if he'd told her who he really was, and since I didn't want to mess it up, I kept my mouth shut.

Courtney placed a hand on his arm. "Come sit down. I'll get you something to drink."

We all moved over to the shiny red counter while she disappeared into the back room, no doubt to grab a bottle of water for him.

"Did you tell her that you're a time traveler?" I asked as soon as she was out of earshot.

"I tried, but she didn't really believe me."

"Maybe this will help convince her," I said.

Courtney returned and handed him the drink. "Tell me

who this man is."

"From 1971 to 1972, Raymond Gonzalez left behind a trail of bodies from Ohio to Virginia—or at least we thought it was him. The FBI was able to capture and question him, but he had an alibi for every death. In the end, we had to let him go. However, I was convinced he had done a lot more than just murder people. He destroyed lives."

"You had no idea he was the skeleton in the wall?" I asked.

"No. How could I? Like I told you, I've never been to Witch's Cove before."

"What about your FBI partners?" Jaxson asked. "Would one of them have followed this man here and killed him?"

"I don't think so. I was the only one assigned to follow him. When no other bodies showed up for a while, I was reassigned to the job of investigating Michael Hamstead. However, it was right after that the FBI located Raymond and brought him in for questioning."

That was bad timing. "Now that we have an identification, the sheriff will need to contact the FBI. Since we more or less know the date of his death, they might be able to learn if any one of the agents followed him after his release," I said. "And then killed him here in Witch's Cove."

"It's possible, but my boss would have told me about it. Regardless, go ahead and ask."

Courtney slid onto the stool next to him. "What you told me was true? You time traveled here?"

"Yes, but don't ask me how. Not even Glinda seems to have any idea how that happened."

"Wow. I know this will sound like a rather odd question,

but exactly what time of day did you arrive in Witch's Cove?"

He looked over at us. He didn't have a cell phone, and if he was wearing a watch, I doubt he thought to look at it. That meant he had no idea about time, so I answered. "Jaxson and I were about to go out to dinner about two weeks ago. As we approached the door, Dominic popped up—if that is the right word."

Courtney glanced to the side. "Dom, what were you doing a few seconds before you arrived in our time?"

His cheeks stained red. "I was packing to go back to Virginia. Why?"

There was more to it than that. The words of Courtney's fortune teller came back to me. "Tell her the truth. I have a feeling it might explain your sudden appearance."

"It's silly," he said. For the first time since his arrival, Dominic acted embarrassed.

"Fine." I turned to Courtney. "Tell Dominic what the fortune teller told you."

She huffed out a slight smile. "For real?"

I wanted to shake both of them. "Do you want me to state what I think?"

"Yes," they said in unison.

Sheesh. "In short, a fortune teller told Courtney to move from Ohio to Florida to find love. She chose to move to Witch's Cove because she liked the name. Personally, I think it was something more than that—something inside her that drew her here." I held up a hand to stop the questions that were sure to come. "As for Dominic, when Jaxson, Rihanna, Iggy, and I time traveled back to Ohio last December and met him, I had thought at the time it had been my sprig of mistletoe that had created the magic."

"Mistletoe?" Courtney's eyes grew wide.

That's what she focused on—not that we'd time traveled? Maybe she had bought into the idea more than I believed.

"It was Christmas. When I was in the middle of kissing Jaxson under the mistletoe, we teleported to Ohio. Naturally, I thought that sprig had caused it. It turned out, it had been a gold coin I'd found that had done the trick."

"Dominic didn't tell me that you all had time traveled." Courtney's mouth opened. Apparently, it had taken a moment for the information to sink in.

"I didn't think it was my place," Dominic said.

For the purpose of time—no pun intended—I had skipped a lot of steps in my explanation. "I'll tell you the whole story later, but for now we need to focus. Dominic found my half-eaten mistletoe that Iggy had destroyed, but that's beside the point. When Dominic spotted it, he sighed, mentally wishing he had the kind of love Jaxson and I have. Correct me if I'm wrong, but I'm betting you, Courtney, were wishing the same thing at the same time." I'd heard of simultaneous wishes coming true once before.

She clamped a hand over her mouth. "I did a lot more than that."

Now it was my turn to be surprised. "What did you do?"

"I did a love spell."

"You are a witch then." I knew it. "You could have told me you were one. It wasn't like I was going to judge you."

Courtney glanced over at Dominic. "I never told anyone. It was why I came here. I thought the people in Witch's Cove might be more receptive should anyone find out."

"They will be." I turned to Dominic. "I have the sense you have no idea that you are a warlock?"

He laughed. "Lady, there is nothing magical about me."

Dom sounded sincere, but he couldn't have been more wrong. "Did you know that only those with magical talents can talk to familiars?"

"What are familiars?"

Oh, boy. "Iggy is one."

Dominic looked over at Jaxson. "Are you a witch, too? You can communicate with Iggy."

"No. Glinda, put a spell on me that thankfully hasn't worn off. It allows me to communicate with Iggy. That's all. By the way, only women are witches. Men are warlocks."

"I stand corrected. Is there anything else you can do?" He addressed my boyfriend.

Jaxson pressed his lips together. "Glinda once performed another spell on me that gave me incredible eyesight and hearing, but it has worn off."

We were getting off topic. "Bottom line, I think that when Courtney did her spell to find the man of her dreams, and Dominic wished to have a relationship like the one Jaxson and I have, something happened. Here's the thing. Even if you both have magical powers, it seems strange that these wishes crossed the continuum of time. Something bigger is at stake here."

"Like what?" Courtney asked.

"I have no idea, but I have a feeling that this skeleton might have something to do with it," I said.

"How can we find out?" Dominic asked. "It's not like I can go to the FBI and tell them the manhunt can now stop, because the body was found fifty years into the future."

Jaxson touched my hand. "We need to tell Steve."

"Our sheriff is not going to believe us that Dominic recognized someone from fifty years ago," I said.

"Then tell him the truth. Tell him that Dom is a time traveler from the seventies," Jaxson said.

"I'm not sure he'll believe me, even though he knows we went back in time six months ago."

"Try him. You've been able to convince him of all the other crazy stuff. Think about werewolves. He was skeptical at first."

"Werewolves are real?" Courtney asked.

"Yes, but most around here are good." I would leave that tale for a girls' night out discussion.

"Suppose we talk to your sheriff," Dominic said. "How does that help? Gonzalez died fifty years ago. Whoever killed him would either be in a totally different state, rotting in jail for committing another crime, or dead."

"It might not help at all, but I always let our sheriff know the progress of a case."

"He won't turn me into the FBI, will he?"

"Probably not, but I imagine Steve would want to do a little research to see if there was a Dominic Geno from Virginia back in the 70s, but that's all. I'll ask him to keep quiet about your existence."

"He'll find a Dominic Geno all right, but I can't prove I'm that guy. I have no identification, remember? In the end, it probably doesn't matter. Heck, I'm betting your sheriff doesn't believe in time travel."

"As Jaxson reminded me, Steve has surprised us in the

past."

Jaxson tapped the counter. "Something has been bothering me, and I couldn't put my finger on it until now."

My boyfriend always had great instincts. "What is it?"

"Remember when we time traveled to Ohio, we found ourselves dressed in winter coats, boots, and jeans."

"Yes, but it was cold out."

"I know, but they weren't *our* clothes. We were dressed in the time period. And when we returned, nothing of what we were wearing came with us."

"I remember. So?" I asked.

"When Dominic suddenly appeared in our office, he was still wearing his 1970's garb. How do you explain it?"

I hadn't thought about it before. "You're right. We were never out of style. It might mean Dom's arrival had nothing to do with Madam Criant, as Gertrude suspected."

"Who's Madam Criant?" Courtney asked.

"The psychic responsible for our time travel."

"Regardless of how Dominic got here—whether it was due to a fluke of magic or because of some random psychic—we should share the name of the skeleton with Steve," Jaxson said.

Dominic nodded. "Now that I've had a moment to think about it, I would feel better if I told someone of authority."

"Let's do it," Jaxson said.

After Dominic told Courtney he'd check back with her later, the three of us headed over to the sheriff's department. I really hoped that Steve didn't laugh at us. Best case, if we gave him the name of the skeleton, he might be able to tell us more about this man, and how he ended up in Witch's Cove.

# Chapter Nine

PEARL'S EYES WIDENED as we stepped into the sheriff's office. To say she gave Dominic the once over would be an understatement. My chatty aunt must have told her about the newcomer. Since both women knew about our Christmas adventure, I had no doubt my aunt told Pearl about Dominic's similar time travel experience.

"Is Steve in by any chance?" I asked as calmly as I could.

"He is."

I wanted to ask if she'd told her grandson about Dominic, but I refrained. We'd find out soon enough. "Great."

When we entered his office, Steve was standing behind his desk waiting for us. From his intense perusal of Dominic, his grandmother had spilled the beans.

"Is it true? You actually came from the past?"

Dominic stood soldier straight. "Yes, sir."

"Have a seat. I'm highly intrigued. But first, tell me how can I help you."

Between the three of us, we told Steve what had happened, though I wasn't convinced he totally believed us.

"You're saying this skeleton is a man the FBI hunted fifty years ago?" Steve asked.

He wanted to know about that and not how time travel

worked? Maybe he did believe me that our Christmas adventure had been real.

"Yes." Dominic motioned to my phone. I pulled up the image of the reconstruction and handed it him. "This is the man I was after fifty years ago." He showed my cell to Steve. "His name was Raymond Gonzalez. Even after the FBI captured and questioned him, we had to let him go due to lack of evidence tying him to the deaths of four people. I knew, in my heart, he was guilty, though." Dominic detailed the deaths, including the fact that the medical examiner was stumped as to how they all died.

I sunk back in my chair. "Steve, you do realize what this means, don't you?"

"Not really. What?"

"This guy. This Raymond Gonzalez was a warlock. He killed his victims with spells."

"Like what happened to Gavin's dad?" Steve asked.

"Yes, it was why the FBI had to let him go."

Steve looked at Dominic. "What did your medical examiner put as the cause of death then?"

"The victims were categorized as dying due to an unknown cause. The ME suspected poison, but nothing in the data bases matched what was in their bodies. We didn't have the super high tech that you have now."

"Technology or not, death by magic leaves very strange traces or no trace at all." I would have to tell him about those deaths later.

Someone knocked on the door. "Sheriff, Gertrude Poole really needs to speak with you."

We would continue this conversation later, which was

okay since Raymond Gonzalez wasn't going anywhere.

She came in and looked around. "Good, you are all here. Please stay seated. I need to talk to all of you."

How did she know we were speaking with the sheriff? Since it was Gertrude, psychic extraordinaire, I shouldn't be surprised.

Jaxson gave up his chair and then went into the main room and dragged in another one. I couldn't even hazard a guess as to what Gertrude wanted to speak to us and the sheriff about.

"How can I help you, Gertrude?" Steve asked.

"I've dreaded this day for fifty years."

Fifty years? Wait a minute. Did she know Raymond Gonzalez after all? Had her memory returned?

"Go on," the sheriff urged.

"In order to fully explain, I need to go back many, many years."

Steve pulled out his yellow note pad. "Okay. Tell me."

"I was living in Witch's Cove at the time, while my good friend, Bethany Criant, was in Ohio minding her own business. Glinda, Jaxson, Rihanna, and Dominic have all met her. It's what enabled some of them to time travel. But I digress. My friend was very powerful, which was probably why Raymond was drawn to her. She sensed his evil nature the moment he approached her, so when he pretended to court her, she turned him down."

"Did she kill him in self-defense?" I hadn't meant to blurt that out.

"Not then."

Not then? But later? Right here in Witch's Cove maybe?

O-kay. "Please, continue."

"For months, she put off his advances. In an attempt to impress her, Raymond would show her what a powerful warlock he was. After all, women like powerful men or so he believed."

I could see where this was going. "Did his show of power include murder?"

"I'm afraid so. When Bethany met Evan, the man she was to marry, Raymond backed off. Temporarily."

Something seemed off in her story, but I didn't want to interrupt her. She often delayed the punch line until later.

"That would be the end of 1972," Dominic said. "I had lost track of him at that time. A few months later the FBI found him."

"That must have been why Bethany called me in a panic, saying Raymond was back."

"Where was Evan?"

Gertrude wove her fingers together. "Safely at home. Even though Evan was not a warlock, he wanted to try to stop this man. Bethany begged him not to interfere, saying she would find a way to deal with him. Thankfully, Evan listened."

"If he hadn't, he might have died." I said it more to myself.

"I'm afraid so."

"What happened next?" Steve asked.

"Bethany drove down to see me. She would have flown, but she didn't want anyone to find her."

My heart was beating hard, the horror of it all so terrible. "Did she tell Evan she was leaving?" I asked.

"Yes, she told her husband that she was coming to see me.

Since we were friends, it made sense. Bethany was a total mess by the time she arrived. It wasn't more than two days later when she sensed Raymond had come to town."

"You're sure he meant to harm her?" Steve asked.

"Absolutely. I've unfortunately lost the letters Raymond sent her, but in them he said he'd kill her if she didn't send him back in time."

Wait a minute. He wanted her to send him back in time? How had I missed that important piece of the puzzle?

"Why did he want to return so badly?" Dominic asked, acting as if it was an everyday occurrence for someone to make that request.

"I'll get to that in a moment," she said.

"How did he learn she had the ability to help people time travel?" I should have let her go at her own pace, but I'd lost my patience.

"I don't know. Clearly, he found out somehow. It was when you all arrived in Charlotte that he returned to demand Bethany do as he asked once more."

"I feel terrible if we had anything to do with him killing anyone."

"You didn't. Bethany had helped others go back in time to right a wrong, which was what Raymond wanted to do. Only the purpose of his trip was to kill his father before his dad took Raymond's mom's life."

My head spun. "Whoa. He wanted to go back in time to kill someone? When Madam Criant told him no, he killed a bunch of people instead? That makes no sense."

"I know. He said that if she wanted to stop further deaths, she had to help him."

I thought he was trying to court her. Clearly, that had been a ruse to get close to her so she'd do as he asked. I'm glad he failed.

"What exactly happened when he arrived in Witch's Cove?" Steve asked.

I was happy one of us could keep the story going in the right direction.

"He threatened her once more. Had we not done something, Raymond would have killed her. I'm sure of it. Mind you, she'd tried many spells over the months to take away his powers, but nothing worked. He was just that strong. After some research, we found a spell that would stop his heart, but only if the two of us worked together."

"You and Bethany Criant killed Raymond Gonzalez?" Steve's composure cracked a bit.

"Yes. I've been guilt-ridden for fifty years because of it, even though the man deserved it. To be honest, it was almost a blessing when Dominic showed up. When I conducted a séance with Bethany, she told me that I had to come clean."

Easy for Madam Criant to say. She couldn't be prosecuted. Though I doubt any court would say Gertrude Poole was guilty. Witchcraft has never been recognized. It stacked up there with voodoo.

Steve blew out a breath and leaned back in his chair. "As far as I know, magic is not against the law. Even though Glinda's necklace confirmed this man died of magic, there is no evidence that points to you, Gertrude, as the killer—or to your friend either."

That was so great of Steve not to pursue legal action. If push came to shove, she could claim self-defense.

"Thank you," Gertrude said. "I can't tell you how relieved I am to hear that."

"Can I ask how you managed to stuff a man in a wall?" Jaxson asked.

"That was not our finest moment, but we were desperate. We hypnotized two strong men to carry the body into the new construction site and seal up the wall. I figured Bethany and I would be long dead before he was ever found."

That was an amazing story. "I guess the case is closed, right?" Please say yes.

"I'm satisfied," Steve said. "I don't think my report even needs to mention Raymond Gonzalez's name."

"Thank you, Sheriff Rocker. Next time I contact Bethany, I will tell her the good news." Gertrude stood, looking a few years younger.

Since this case was officially over, there was no need to continue the discussion. Jaxson and I made sure she returned safely to her office while Dominic went back to the candy store to fill Courtney in on what had happened. Never in a million years would I have expected Gertrude to end a man's life.

"We need to get back to the office," I said. "Assuming Iggy's back from his wanderings, he'll be upset we took so long."

"The moment you tell him what happened, he'll forget about any slight he feels."

I smiled. "That's probably true."

When we entered the office, Iggy was on the coffee table. "What took you so long?" If he could press his lips together in defiance, he would have.

"Do we have something juicy to tell you." Juicy was Iggy's favorite word.

I went into the kitchen to fix drinks while Jaxson began the discussion of how Raymond Gonzalez came to be stuffed in the candy store wall. I returned with the drinks, and Iggy was staring up at Jaxson with total attention.

I sat down, and even though I heard Jaxson's retelling of what went down, it was hard to believe.

"I never thought Gertrude could be a murderer," Iggy said. "I gotta watch what I say in front of her."

"Iggy! She's not some serial killer. She had to stop the man from murdering her best friend."

Jaxson picked up his drink. "This makes me want to find out more about this Raymond Gonzalez guy and see what the press said about him."

"I'm curious, too. I want to know if anyone speculated that two witches did him in." I'm sure that wouldn't have happened, but it would be interesting to learn what the gossips of the time had to say about the man's disappearance, assuming they had been aware he had even been in town.

We both moved over to the computer. Now that Jaxson knew the identity of the skeleton, it was easier to find information on him. I suppose we could have asked Steve to investigate, but our sheriff had more important things to do.

"Here's something," Jaxson said.

We both read the report. "He lived in Hilltop, Ohio. I wonder how far that is from Charlotte, not that it matters, but I like to understand where everything is located," I said.

He did a map search. "Pretty far. It's on the other side of the state."

"I wonder how he met Bethany then?"

"Good question," Jaxson said. "We need Dominic to fill in the blanks for us."

"Totally. I'm sure as an FBI agent, he would have done a thorough background check on Raymond if he was a person of interest in a serial murder case." As if I'd summoned him, Dominic came into the office. I turned around. "What did Courtney think of Gertrude's confession?"

"She was blown away." He stuck his hand in his pocket.

Iggy crawled up his leg. "Whatcha got there?"

Dominic looked down, smiled, and scooped up Iggy into the crux of his arm. "It's a gem. One of the workers found this in the wall that faced the back room." He held out a blue stone.

I pushed back my chair, stood, and walked over to him to get a better look at it. As I approached, a blast of heat seared my chest where my pendant was resting. As I clasped my necklace, my vision turned white, and I felt as if I was falling. "Something is happening to me," I choked out as my hearing faded and my equilibrium faltered.

Jaxson rushed over and wrapped an arm around my waist. "Glinda?"

Dominic grabbed one of my shoulders with his free hand. What was going on? I let out a breath, and when I opened my eyes, I expected to be staring into Dominic's face. Instead, everything had changed, and my pulse skyrocketed.

"Where are we?" Okay, I kind of knew, since I'd been there before. "I mean, I recognize this as Madam Criant's shop, but how did we get here?"

In truth, the bigger question was what year was it? It had

to be in the past, right? Madam Criant was dead in our time, which meant her store wouldn't look the same or even exist.

"Glinda? Jaxson? Mr. Geno. What are you doing here?" The sixty-four thousand dollar question came from Bethany— still a middle-aged Madam Criant. Oh, drat. We'd traveled back in time. Again.

"You didn't send us?" I asked.

"No, dear. I didn't."

# *Chapter Ten*

THIS WASN'T GOOD. Even when Bethany had helped us with the time travel before, it had been hard enough to return to the present, but to do so again, might be impossible.

"What's the month and year?" I asked, keeping my fingers crossed she wouldn't say 1972.

Bethany Criant's brows pinched. "It's May, 1973."

Ugh. That was just as bad.

"That's when I left Charlotte—or rather was about to leave," Dominic said.

"Interesting. Glinda, I am more interested in how you and Jaxson ended up here *with* Dominic?" She waved a hand. "How about I fix some tea and you can tell me what is going on?"

How could she sound so calm? What did she know that we didn't?

Just then Iggy crawled out of Dominic's grasp. "I love this place," my little familiar said.

I couldn't remember if he'd been to her store the last time we were here or if he'd even been introduced to Madam Criant. Most likely, when Jaxson, Rihanna, and Iggy had been stuck back here, Madam Criant had met my mischievous familiar.

Dominic huffed. "I'm sorry, but I'm confused. Again. What just happened?"

He'd been shuttled from one time period to another. Twice now. That would upset anyone. This being my third time-traveling experience, I wasn't as disoriented.

"I can't be sure, but I experienced the same dizziness as before when we time traveled back here. It must have been something I did. Why we returned to this town again, I don't know."

"The blue stone seemed to have been the key," Jaxson offered.

"You might be right. When I came close to the stone, my necklace heated up. The two must have interacted some- how—or so I'm guessing."

"Glinda?" Jaxson stepped closer and clasped my shoulders. "It's gone."

"What's gone?"

His gaze dropped to my chest. "Your necklace. Remember the last time it didn't travel with you either, because your grandmother only gave it to you a few years ago."

My knees weakened. "Then how are we to get back?" Reason quickly intruded. "Let's hope Madam Criant can give us a bit of help like she did the last time."

Bethany Criant breezed in from the back carrying a tray of tea. Like before, she had my pink cup, Jaxson's mug, a delicate, flowered porcelain cup that she used, and a dark blue mug for Dominic, a color that was befitting an FBI agent.

"Please, have a seat."

She placed the tray on the low table. The only seats were the beanbag chairs, which was fine by me since they were incredibly comfortable.

I sat down, picked up my tea, and sipped it. "Delicious." It had just the right amount of sugar. Somehow, she knew my preference.

"Got any lettuce?" Iggy asked.

I laughed, mostly out of embarrassment. "Oh, Iggy. It's rude to ask."

"No, it's not. I just might have something for our weary traveler." Our psychic disappeared once more and returned a moment later with a hibiscus flower. "Here you go, young man."

"Thank you. You are the best."

I was happy he was appreciative, but it was almost as if she knew we were coming. Why else would she have a hibiscus flower in her psychic shop? I didn't want to think that she could create things with her mind, like those food replicators in science fiction television shows.

She sat down. "I think I know what might have happened. I've been having these strange, vivid dreams. I now suspect it had something to do with your arrival." She looked over at Dominic. "I am quite confused why you are here, though. You are from this time."

I was a bit discouraged that she hadn't been aware he'd traveled to and from Witch's Cove. And her having dreams about us shouldn't be what sent us back in time. At least, I hoped that wasn't all it took.

"I am, but I'll let Glinda give you the rundown. I think she understands it the best."

"I'm not so sure I do, but I'll try."

I began with meeting our new candy store owner. When I

mentioned Courtney Higgins' name, Madam Criant didn't react, implying they weren't psychically connected in any way. "To our horror, one of the workers found a skeleton in the wall of her shop."

"How terrible." She acted as if she had no idea about the existence of the skeleton. On second thought, maybe she didn't know. Raymond's murder might have not happened yet.

"We were all pretty traumatized."

"Turns out, the skeleton was—" Dominic started to say, but I held up a hand.

"We'll get to that in a moment."

"Sure. Sorry."

I was happy he understood, especially since Madam Criant was being stalked by this man, she'd know him. Jaxson, Dominic, and I told our tale about how Dominic just appeared in our office.

"That must have been a quite the shock," she said to Dom.

"Tell me about it. Had I not recognized Glinda and Jaxson, I don't know what I would have done. To be honest, until Jaxson told me what year it was, I hadn't even realized I had traveled to the future. It was all very disorienting. What was just as startling was how much the world had changed in only fifty years. I didn't even know there were laptops or cell phones, but they are remarkable inventions."

"I don't know what those are either," she said.

"It's all future tech stuff." We didn't need to get off track. "Dominic was lucky he saw a friendly face. I can't imagine arriving in Charlotte and not having had Jaxson and Rihanna with me."

"I was there," Iggy said.

I smiled. "Yes, you were. I would have freaked out if you hadn't been with me. Anyway, since Dominic was anxious to return to his time, we asked Gertrude for help."

"I don't think she's ever done any time travel. That was always my specialty."

I nodded. "So I found out. She had no idea how or why he'd arrived, which was why we had a séance to ask you about it."

She looked off to the side. "That means I'm dead in your time."

Oh, drat. Me and my big mouth. I hadn't even considered that. "You'd only died recently," I said, though I wasn't sure that would help.

"We all have to go at some point, I guess," she said with resignation.

For the daughter of a funeral director, I should have been more sympathetic. "We do." I cleared my throat. "While there, we asked Gertrude if she knew the identity of the skeleton, and she said she didn't know who he was even though my magical pendant insisted this man had been killed with magic."

"Why would she know?"

Because you two killed him, but that, too, would be in the future. "I thought she might have heard of a man who'd gone missing many years ago."

"I see."

From the lack of any kind of emotional response, I don't think she had a clue who the man was. Too bad Gertrude hadn't remembered the year. Or maybe she had and hadn't wanted to tell us.

"Eventually, the clay representation of the face came back from another lab." Now, I nodded to Dominic. I'd let him do the big reveal since he'd been the one to track this terrible man. "Your turn."

"I recognized the face as that of Raymond Gonzalez."

As much as I wished Rihanna had been here with us, I didn't need a mind reader to know what Madam Criant was thinking.

She planted a hand on her chest. "How can that be?"

Now came the hard part. "You might find this difficult to believe, but it is the truth. Gertrude confessed to killing him, together with you, because he'd threatened your life."

She sipped on her tea, acting as if we'd told her it was going to rain tomorrow.

"When was this?" Her voice sounded calm, but her hand shook so hard, she had to put down her drink.

"We don't know. Gertrude couldn't remember the date or the year."

"Did she say how we killed him?" Bethany swallowed hard.

I was thankful she didn't call us liars. "Kind of. The two of you had to join together in order to do a spell to stop his heart. Individually, your powers weren't enough."

I found it surprising that anyone who could send people through time lacked the ability to harm another—powerful warlock or not—but apparently that had been the case.

She picked up her cup once more and held it to her chest. "Are you saying all the spells I plan to do to take away his powers won't work?"

"I might have said too much already. If you know the future, you might change your actions, which could affect what occurs after that." I had no idea if that was true, but it seemed logical.

"It could, but did Gertrude tell you why Raymond had to die?"

"He'd killed four people that we know of," Dominic said.

"Four? I was only aware of three."

Three was bad enough.

"The FBI is suspecting it is even more," Dominic said.

Bethany grunted as if in pain. "I read that he'd been caught by the FBI. It was such a joyous day, which quickly turned to tragedy two days later, when I found out he'd been released."

"After meeting Glinda, I realized that Raymond killed these people using magic. I now believe they died a day or two later, because of a spell he performed. This delay gave him time to have an alibi. It was why he had to be released. We had no proof of his crimes."

She clamped her jaw tighter. "That's something he would have done. It's my fault though."

"No, it's not," Dominic said. "You didn't kill anyone."

"I know, but if I had sent him back in time to kill his father like he asked, none of the other people would have had to die."

What a terrible dilemma. My mind raced. "Gertrude said that Raymond knew you could help people time travel because of us, right?" Or had I not remembered correctly?

"Not exactly. I had helped several people return to their

past to right a wrong long before you. While they promised not to tell anyone, Raymond learned about it somehow. People talk, you know."

"Tell me about it."

"He stopped by my store about three months ago, because he'd heard about your exploits and became even more demanding. He even threatened to kill people I cared about if I didn't do as he asked."

"What a monster." I imagine I'd never know how he'd learned we were time travelers. No one knew but Bethany, and she wouldn't have told anyone—or so I hoped. I turned to Dominic. "Could the two of you share the names of the people Bethany helped leap the time continuum with the people you believed Gonzalez murdered?" Since Dominic had been on the case, he probably had memorized every name. "I'm wondering if there is any overlap."

"Of course," Dominic said. "Bethany, if you have a piece of paper, I'll write down the names."

As she stood, the psychic seemed to age before my eyes. When she retreated to her secret back room, Jaxson leaned over. "What are you thinking?"

"That Raymond found out about one of the people who'd time traveled and either tortured them for Bethany's name or asked them how she'd done it."

Jaxson's eyes widened. "I am impressed. Good thinking."

I loved his praise. "Thank you."

As soon as Bethany returned with paper and pencil, Dominic and she proceeded to make a list. If there wasn't at least one name that matched, I wasn't sure how we would proceed from there.

About a minute later, they compared names. Dominic's face paled. "I can't believe it."

The suspense was killing me. "What?"

"All but one of the names of those murdered matched her list, but Bethany has three more names, including both of yours."

I grabbed Jaxson's hand while Iggy pranced up to Dominic. "Is my name on the list?"

Really?

"No, my little one," Madam Criant said. "I also didn't write down Rihanna's name either since I know she is safe in the future. But Iggy, if you should meet him, don't say a word, or he'll know you are magical."

His eyes widened, if that was possible, and then he nodded.

I couldn't believe this. It wasn't safe for us here. "How can we stop him?"

"That's the problem," Dom said. "Like I said, when the FBI brought him in for questioning, we had no real proof of him killing anyone. Even if we brought him in again, he'd walk."

This was depressing, but there had to be something we could do. "Both Bethany and I are witches. If we join forces, maybe we can do a spell to stop him. That would depend, however, on whether we can find Raymond Gonzalez."

"Raymond comes and goes. It's always unexpected and unwelcome," Bethany said.

"You said he came to your store the last time. Has he ever stopped at your house?"

"No, thankfully, but I've warned Evan about him. I made

him promise not to try to take Raymond down. My husband is not a warlock. He wouldn't stand a chance against someone as powerful as Raymond Gonzalez."

That matched what she told Gertrude in the future.

"Glinda just told me I'm a warlock since I can hear Iggy. Maybe I can help. Three people joining forces instead of two might be better."

Bethany shook her head. "That is nice of you to offer, but I've heard that when a person passes through a time portal, they might pick up some warlock tendencies."

"Hearing Iggy is my only talent then?" Dominic sounded disappointed.

"Perhaps," she said.

"We could try training him and see." At this point, I was willing to do anything.

"We could, but that would take a long time. We need to think of something else," she said.

This was getting worse by the minute. "Dominic, it seems as if Raymond has not struck in the last few months. Is that right?"

He looked over his list. "You're right. He might be laying low for now. I imagine being caught by the FBI shook him, warlock or no warlock."

I turned to Bethany. "Gonzalez will be asking you again to help him at some point in the future."

"He already did, which was why I had planned to seek Gertrude's council."

And kill him. Roger that.

# Chapter Eleven

"YOU CAN'T," I blurted out.

"Can't what? Visit my friend in Witch's Cove?" Bethany asked.

"Yes, or rather, no. You can visit, but you shouldn't, at least not before Raymond is no longer a threat." I wanted to prevent her and Gertrude from having to murder Raymond. I wanted him captured, dead, or powerless before that.

Her chuckle came out rueful. "I thought we'd established he can't be stopped—at least when I am by myself. You and I could join forces, but are you certain you are as powerful as Gertrude?"

Hardly. "No, I'm not." I looked up at Dominic. "Show her the stone. Maybe we can use this gem to send Raymond back to his hometown in another time—like to a year after his mother has already been murdered. And then we could leave him there. I thought it might be better if we did the sending, though. You don't need any more guilt."

"You wouldn't feel bad?"

"It isn't like we'd be killing him."

She held out her hand. "Let me see that gem."

Dominic handed the stone to her. Since I didn't have my pink pendant, nothing should happen to us.

Bethany studied it. "It looks ordinary, but I can feel something pulsing inside it. It's possible someone powerful put a spell on it." She shook her head. "I don't think this could help send him back. It might need your companion necklace, Glinda."

"Fine, then just use your gold coin."

"I could do that."

She was hesitating. Why? What was I missing? "Considering Dominic didn't age when he came forward in time, I'm assuming that if you sent Raymond back in time—or someone did—that he would be a forty something year-old man and not a kid, right?"

"That's right."

"Which means that as a man, he'd have the ability to kill his dad."

"Unfortunately."

Darn. There had to be another option. I just needed to think of it. "Can we send him somewhere beside his hometown? Maybe to another country but not provide him with any money so he'd have a hard time getting back. It could even be in this time period."

She leaned forward. "I guess it's possible, but time travel is complicated. It doesn't always work as planned. Sending you from Witch's Cove to here was rather easy. There seems to be a portal in your town. I suspect it's because of the many witches present. Here's the thing, though. Once a person breaches the fabric of time, it weakens it. With each passage, the next one is easier."

Great. Just our luck the portal was in our office or so it seemed. "Does that mean if we time traveled back and forth a few times from Witch's Cove to here that someone might *accidentally* come through—for lack of a better word?"

"I don't have enough experience to say, but it seems like it could happen."

That was a really scary thought. I looked over at Jaxson. "I have a really, really, crazy idea."

He laughed. "Pink lady, most of your ideas are crazy, but for some unknown reason, they work. Tell me."

"I have had a few thoughts, but most have tiny issues associated with them. Hopefully, one of you can suggest a fix."

"Like what?" Jaxson asked.

"We know the identities of two of the time travelers that Raymond hasn't killed yet—you and me. If Raymond spots us in town, we could have Dominic follow him and then take a movie of him creating a potion. We could stop him before he succeeds in saying the curse and then show the video to the FBI."

"No! That is unacceptable." Jaxson practically shouted.

"I agree with Jaxson, Glinda," Dominic said. "Not only could it go terribly wrong, the FBI doesn't believe in magic. Even if we filmed Raymond saying a spell that would harm you, no court would convict him of attempted murder."

"That was my tiny issue. The same result would happen in our time."

"Got a better idea?" Jaxson asked.

"My second thought—which I discarded rather quickly— was that Bethany and I could do that heart-stopping spell that worked in the future, but as she pointed out, the flaw is that I'm not as powerful as Gertrude."

Jaxson shrugged. "Maybe we could ask Gertrude to time travel here."

I looked over at Bethany. "Could we do that?"

"I suppose, but if we kill him in Witch's Cove in the near future, we might have better luck sticking with that plan. After all, we got away with it there until after I'd died, and Gertrude was old."

She was right. "Fine. I didn't think you would go for it anyway, but here is one that might work."

Iggy jumped between us. "I know. You're going to say that I save the day. Right?"

If only. "Do you have a plan?"

"I'm powerful. Maybe the three of us could send that monster someplace really hot."

I hoped he meant Florida. "Go on."

"Why doesn't Bethany go back in time and convince Raymond's mother to leave town because her husband plans to kill her?" Iggy finally explained. "That way Raymond's mom won't die, and he won't need to take revenge."

I was about to laugh until I realized that his idea could work. I waited for someone to say it was a stupid idea, but the room remained eerily silent.

"It has potential," Bethany said.

A quick shot of excitement raced through me, until the logistics of doing Iggy's plan crashed down on me. "What if she says no? She might not believe us that her husband plans to kill her."

"Glinda is right," Jaxson said. "Not only that, I personally think it is too dangerous. The father might catch wind of the plan and kill not only the messenger but his young son." He turned to me. "Didn't you say Dr. Sanchez found that Raymond had suffered from two spiral arm fractures, which implied abuse?"

"I'm afraid so."

"That's horrible," Bethany said. "He never told me. I only knew that his father killed his mother."

I needed to find a plan we could all live with. "Let's suppose Daddy dearest doesn't learn of the plan. If Raymond's mom says she doesn't believe her husband is evil, we could show her evidence of her death to convince her. Surely you, Dom, can access the crime scene files. If Raymond's father did indeed kill the mother, then there would be images of her body."

"I could show her a photo of her dead, but remember her body had no marks on it, which was why they couldn't catch him. She'll think she died of natural causes."

"Darn. You're right. Any other ideas?" I looked around.

"Let me see what I can find out about the case," Dominic said. "I agree that saving both mother and son might be our best chance to change history."

"If we do try to alter the past, we'd have to make sure the father doesn't find them," Jaxson said. "Ever."

"That could be a problem." Bethany had been quiet for a while. "If Raymond is a powerful warlock, it's highly probable the father is also one. I'm betting the mom has no powers, because if she did, she probably would have escaped already. What scares me is that the dad might have special powers to track his wife no matter where you put her. Her death might be worse than what really happened."

"There has to be something we can do," Jaxson said.

"Can you find out if she has any family she can stay with? I realize that might be the first place her husband looks though." I turned to Bethany. "Hypothetically, suppose the wife was murdered on say, July 1st. If we make sure she is still alive on July 2nd, does that mean the murder never happened, nor would ever happen?"

Bethany sipped her tea, clearing trying to search her mind to find the answer. "That is an excellent question. Sad to say, I don't know."

I bet Levy might be able to find out, even though he claimed he was unfamiliar with time travel. "Do you know of anyone who would know for sure?"

"No, I don't discuss my abilities with others. In fact, I couldn't tell you who is and who isn't a witch or warlock in Charlotte. I envy you and Gertrude. You have a support system."

"We do."

Jaxson set his mug on the table. "I don't think we should do anything rash since we don't have all of the facts. Rushing often spells disaster."

"I have to agree with Jaxson," Dominic said. "The FBI pounded it into us that we needed to be sure of our surroundings before we proceeded."

"We need a new tactic. Dominic is back where he wants to be. At least we've accomplished something on this trip. I think Glinda, Iggy, and I should return to our time in order to do more research. Assuming you can give us one of those gold coins to return, that is," Jaxson said to Bethany.

"I could," Bethany said, "but maybe I should come with you since Raymond won't be there."

She just wanted to see Gertrude, and I couldn't blame her. "If Raymond returns to Charlotte—in 1973—and doesn't find you, who's to say he won't try to extract the information from Evan?"

She sucked in a breath. "You're right. If Raymond is willing to kill and kill again to get back in time, he won't stop at anything."

"Are you able to do as he asked and send him back?" I needed to fully understand the situation. "It's not ideal, but one death of a bad person would be better than having Raymond kill more people in the future."

"Even if I tried, it's not like I always get the date right. He could arrive a week after his mother's murder. Time travel isn't pinpoint accurate when it comes to the date."

"Does he know this?" I asked.

"I told him."

"It's not like he could take his revenge out on you if he couldn't get back to this time. Did he ask how he was going to return if you're here?" She could magically send a gold token, like she had for us, but Bethany wouldn't have told him that, I bet.

"I don't think it mattered to him. His goal was only to save his mom. I've never seen anyone care more about one person than Raymond, yet at the same time have so little regard for life."

"If he managed to stop his father from killing his mother, the little eight-year-old boy would grow up with either a mother and a monster for a father, or with no father at all." I wasn't sure I'd ever really understand the nuances of time travel.

"No one has ever grilled me like you, Glinda, and trust me, if I had the answers, I'd tell you. It might be better to return to your time and learn more about the nature of his family dynamics."

"I think we don't have much of a choice but to go back to the present day."

"But I'm going with you," Dominic said.

That didn't surprise me. "I'd love to have you join us, but what if something happens here, and Bethany can't bring you back?"

He stretched out his legs. "I've been giving it a lot of thought. While I like my job with the Bureau, after seeing what the future holds, I'm willing to give up the present."

"Does Courtney have anything to do with it?"

He smiled. "I thought only your cousin read minds."

# Chapter Twelve

"THE SMILE IN your eyes tells me you like her. Besides, you and Courtney seem to be perfect for each other, but I worry every time we travel from one time to another, something could go wrong," I warned.

"I could say the same thing to you."

"I know, but I have Jaxson and Iggy. While I'd miss my family and Rihanna if we couldn't return to our time, I'd adapt."

Jaxson and I leaned over at the same time and shared a kiss.

"Gross," Iggy said.

We all laughed. "Are we in agreement that all of us should return to Witch's Cove in the twenty-first century in order to learn more about what happened to Raymond's father, and maybe even Raymond, after his mother died?"

They all nodded. "It sounds like a good plan."

"When would you like to leave?" Bethany asked.

Iggy pranced over to us. "Does this mean you aren't going back in time to convince Mrs. Gonzalez that she needs to leave her husband?"

I picked up my darling iguana. "Not now. We need to be sure she will believe us before we attempt anything."

"It also will depend on whether we can land in the right place at the right time," Jaxson said.

"Bethany, I wonder if we manage to silence Raymond—or take away his power—on our next trip back, will it change the future so much that Dominic won't be sent to us in the future?"

"Can that happen?" Dominic looked distraught, and I couldn't blame him.

"Those are all good questions, but I honestly don't know the answers. Nor do I know why Courtney was sent to Witch's Cove. Is there some master plan for her to find the skeleton, which will be what draws Dominic there?" she said. "Someone might know, but it's not me."

Dom dragged his fingers down his jaw. "It would be bad if we change things too much. We need to think things through."

"Worst case, you stay here. Think about it. If the future is changed so much that you never traveled to our time, you wouldn't have ever met Courtney," I said. And hence he wouldn't miss her.

"Maybe." Dominic didn't sound convinced.

"Glinda. I'm going to dub you the woman with the infinite questions," Bethany said. "I promise to do more research into time travel. I wish I knew all of the ins and outs, but I don't. Maybe that is why I am so hesitant to send people back or forward in time. All I know is that when we mess with mother nature, there are consequences. Some we can anticipate and others we can't."

I didn't want to ask what kind of consequences. "Has there been a time when you haven't been able to get someone back to their time?"

She pressed her lips together and lowered her gaze. "Once. It was my worst failing. I can only hope they made the best of it."

My stomach grumbled. Go figure. The timing of my cravings was always inconvenient. "Is anyone up for some food?"

Jaxson turned to Dominic. "Glinda is always up for eating."

"I would deny it, but it is true." I turned to Bethany. "Is the River Bend Café still operating?" We'd only been there five months ago, so it should be.

"I don't have a crystal ball, but I'm betting it will never close."

"Good to know."

Jaxson stood. "Over dinner, we can decide what other things we need to research before returning."

I looked around for my purse. "I don't think we have money."

Dominic pulled out his wallet. When he opened it, he smiled. "I do. Dinner is on me."

DURING OUR MEAL, we kept the topic away from time travel and evil warlocks. We didn't need the whole diner learning about Raymond Gonzalez and his murderous streak. One bonus of coming to this eatery was that our server, Sissy, was there. She'd helped us during our Christmas visit. I referred to her as the Dolly Andrews of Charlotte.

"Here's your check," she said after we'd all finished our delicious meal. "It was so good to see you again."

"Thank you. It was nice seeing you too. I have a question for you."

Her eyes lit up. "Shoot."

"Do you know if Raymond Gonzalez is back in town?" I asked. "We need to speak with him.".

She looked at the ceiling. "Raymond Gonzalez? Nope. I can't say that I know him, but someone must. Let me check for you."

Bethany was quick to give her one of her business cards. "You can call me if you find out anything. It's important."

"For sure." She glanced over at Dominic and smiled.

Her look reminded me of how all the Witch's Cove women would look at Jaxson. Thankfully, when that happened, he never flirted back.

Dominic nodded, but I could see he'd already given his heart to Courtney. After he paid, we walked back to Bethany's shop to continue formulating our plan.

We'd just sat down when Bethany blew out a breath. "Are you all still committed to going back to your time?"

"We have to if we want to make sure that Raymond Gonzalez doesn't threaten you, or anyone you care about, again," I said.

"Agreed, but how do you propose we do that exactly?" she asked. "We haven't come up with a good plan other than delving into Raymond's past."

She was right. "Anyone have any ideas?"

We sat in silence for a bit. "We could make him have really bad nightmares," Iggy said as he climbed out of my purse. "He's probably already had a lot of them, especially if he knew his dad killed his mom."

"I know Raymond is an evil man, but he's already in pain over his traumatic childhood." I shouldn't be sympathetic to his plight, but I was—until I remembered that he'd killed so many people in cold blood and had threatened to kill Bethany and those she loved. "On the other hand, he is a serial killer."

Funny that a few hours ago, I had been willing to send him to another country and leave him there. Was giving him nightmares any worse?

Jaxson twisted toward me. "You know how much you don't like to be tickled, right?"

I immediately held up my hands and scooted away. "Don't you dare."

"My point exactly. In fact, you always beg me to stop. You probably would do anything I asked to make it stop, right?"

I didn't know what he was getting at. "Maybe."

"What if we were able to do something to Raymond that was so terrible, he'd do anything to put a halt to it?" Jaxson said.

"Like what?" Dominic asked. "Show him his future self stuffed in the wall of a soon-to-be candy store?"

"Ooh, I like it," I said. "That's like the movie *A Christmas Carol* where there's the ghost of Christmas past, the ghost of Christmas present, and the ghost of Christmas future that shows the person what their life is going to be like if they don't change."

"I wasn't suggesting anything that elaborate, but I'm open," Jaxson said.

Iggy spun around, indicating he had what he thought was a brilliant idea. "Yes, Detective Goodall?"

"That's what I'm talking about. Give him nightmares— really, really bad ones. You could call on the ghosts of the people he'd killed and have them haunt him. They could sound eerie and follow him around all day. They could say how much he'd ruined their lives, and that they won't leave him alone. Ever."

My first instinct was to dismiss what my familiar said, but once more, he'd impressed me. "I love that, but I have no idea how to do it. We'd have to do a lot of séances, and the dead people might not even want to respond."

"Iggy, come here," Madam Criant said.

Iggy crawled over. "You rang?"

She smiled. "You are one smart detective."

"Thank you. I'm glad someone appreciates me."

"I do." She placed him on her lap, which I'm sure he considered a very prestigious position.

"Is what Iggy suggested possible?" I asked.

"I think so, but Gertrude is the expert on ghosts since she does so many séances."

Iggy lifted his head. "I'm an expert. I've communicated with many ghosts. Glinda has some experience, too."

Some? "I have to say the idea of having ghosts haunt Raymond appeals to me."

"What's the end goal?" Dominic asked. "By that, I mean what are you hoping to accomplish?"

We all looked at each other. I wasn't sure.

"He needs to turn himself in and confess his crimes," Jaxson said.

"Would the FBI even believe him if he told them that he put a spell on people that ended up killing them?" I asked. "It's not like he can produce the murder weapon. Not only that, I don't think there is a court for people of magic and shifters like there is in our time."

Dominic blew out a breath. "No. Certainly none I've heard about."

"There is something we can do, though," Bethany said.

My heart beat fast. "What is it?"

"Have one of the ghosts tell him that he has to give dates of when the people died. He'd have to include how he stalked them and why he chose them in particular."

"The FBI might throw him in a mental institution if he said ghosts were talking to him every night," I tossed in. "And if he mentioned the possibility of time travel, for sure they'd send him away."

Bethany almost looked through me. "That confession would take him out of circulation. I'm not sure he'd ever be able to talk his way out of leaving either. Nor am I sure he'd want to. If he tries to convince people to let him go, I could contact the deceased again. I'm sure they'd be happy to bother him night after night after night."

Excitement surged through me. "I'm game." I looked over at Dominic. "What do you think?"

"We have nothing to lose. We should give it a go. I know nothing about ghosts, but if Bethany thinks she can make it happen, then sure."

"Not me, but Gertrude. And maybe Glinda can help," Bethany said.

"I'd be happy to."

Iggy was looking up at me. "Yes? What do you think, Iggy?"

"I want to participate. This could be really fun."

How had I raised such an animal? He disliked dead bodies but loved ghosts. "Absolutely. You're in. Let's do this."

Bethany stood. "Let me prepare for our transport then."

"Prepare?" I was hoping that time travel was merely a matter of rubbing the gold coin with your thumb and making a wish that you were in a different place. It was basically what I did the last time.

"I need to make a potion," she said.

"Go for it." I wanted to watch and learn, but I had a feeling she wouldn't allow me to see what she did.

As soon as she disappeared into the back room, I gathered Iggy. "I don't need you wandering off. It would be terrible if we left you behind."

"Don't worry. This place is cool, but you know I can't survive in the winter."

"You're right."

Bethany eventually returned carrying a rather ordinary-looking bowl. It was covered with a cloth so I couldn't tell if the items inside were whole, mashed, or liquified.

"I've just called Evan and told him that I will go with you for a few days."

"He knows you're going to time travel to the future?" I asked.

"Not exactly. Evan tends to worry too much. I told him I wanted to visit Gertrude."

"You will be. You will see your old friend."

"I know," she said. "Are we ready?"

"You have to say a spell, right?"

She pulled a coin from her pocket. "With this and the herbs, we'll have a nice trip."

One second we were there, and the next we were back in the Pink Iguana Sleuth's office. Jaxson's arm was once more around my waist where it had been the last time we were in Witch's Cove, and Iggy was in Dominic's arm. His other hand was on my shoulder.

Had I just imagined today? "What happened?"

# Chapter Thirteen

DOMINIC MOVED BACK and placed Iggy on the ground. My familiar looked up at me. "I'm worried about you."

"You're worried about me, why?"

"You don't remember what happened? At Madam Criant's? She was really cool."

My shoulders sagged. "I didn't imagine time traveling back to the 1970s then?"

Jaxson looked around. "No, but where is Bethany? She said she was going to come with us."

I looked behind Dominic and blinked a few times, because I swear the outside wall was wavering. "Do you see that?" I pointed to the distortion.

Dominic rushed over and stuck out his hand, as if to check whether his eyes, too, were deceiving him. If I didn't know better, I'd have thought part of his arm disappeared for a moment.

"That is strange," he said in a rather funny voice.

"What is it?"

"I swear my hand started to go through the wall, and then it didn't," Dominic said. "Bethany was right. Time travel can mess with a person."

Without thinking, I touched my necklace. Whenever I

was a bit upset, I liked to hold it. The gem gave me comfort. Only then did I realize that because I was wearing my necklace, we might time travel again. "Dominic, do you have the blue stone?"

"I think so." He placed his hand in his pocket.

As he started to lift his hand, I held up a palm. "Stop. We can't chance both stones being near each other again or we might go back—or forward in time. We need to hide the gem." I looked over at Jaxson. "Any suggestions where the best place might be?"

He looked around the room. "How about Rihanna's room? You just need to make sure you don't go in there unless you remove your necklace first. Or I could take it back to my place. If we needed it, though, it would take a moment to retrieve it."

"Hiding it in Rihanna's room is a good idea for now."

As Dominic moved toward me, I stepped as far from him as possible, and I didn't relax until they disappeared.

Less than a minute later, they both came out of Rihanna's room. "Let's sit down," Jaxson said. "Something is going on here that I don't understand. In fact, I'm more confused than ever about time travel."

"You and me both," I chimed in.

"I understand it," Iggy said.

Since my legs were still shaking from the experience, I had to sit. "Come here and tell us, Iggy."

"Bethany wants you to figure things out yourself, but she'll show up if need be."

"How do you know that, buddy?" Jaxson asked. "Did Bethany telepathically communicate that to you?"

"No, but I can sense these things." He tapped his face with his leg.

"Good to know." I wasn't inclined at the moment to believe him, but my familiar did have a sixth sense. My phone still sat on the table—just where I'd left it, so I checked the time and day. "It seems as if only minutes have elapsed. Once more, time travel has succeeded in confounding me."

"Do you believe Bethany tried to make it, but failed, or is she waiting for the right moment to arrive like Iggy suggested?" Dominic seemed rather upset over Bethany not being here.

"I don't know. We could have passed through the portal one too many times, and she couldn't come."

"Has she been here before?" Dominic asked.

"Not that she's told us. Sheesh. I hope the portal didn't disintegrate completely."

"That would be bad. We need to get back one more time, and this time we need to ask Gertrude to go with us," Iggy said.

Jaxson sighed. "We will go back, buddy, when we're done here, but what if it is too much for Gertrude's body?" He looked up at us. "I personally didn't feel any ill effects, but who's to say it isn't dangerous for an older person?"

I, too, didn't want to do anything that might harm Gertrude. I'd never be able to live with myself. "When we approach her, we'll have to tell her all of the possible side effects."

Before we could discuss anything further, Rihanna breezed in. She looked at each of us and then shrugged off her purse. "You seem different. What happened?"

Different how? Or didn't I want to know? "Have a seat. You won't believe what happened."

She set her bag on the floor, and as soon as she plopped down on the sofa, Iggy jumped onto her lap. "Tell me," she said.

I wasn't sure where to begin, in part because I had to remember when the last time was that we spoke with her. "Did you know we learned the identity of the skeleton?"

"No. Who was it?"

I nodded to Dominic. "A man by the name of Raymond Gonzalez. He was a serial killer who I had followed for quite some time back in the 70's." He went on to explain about us telling Steve who this dead man was.

"Then Gertrude showed up and confessed to killing him," I announced.

"Gertrude? A killer?" Rihanna said. "That can't be."

"She said she and Madam Criant used a spell to kill him." I explained how he'd threatened to kill Bethany if she didn't send him back in time.

"Wow."

"I know, right?"

"Why did this guy want to go back in time?" Rihanna asked.

Just as I was about to explain, footsteps sounded on the stairs. A second later, Drake poked his head up. "What's going on? You all look so serious."

Not that I had a problem telling Drake what had transpired, but I'd like his talented witch girlfriend's opinion on the issue too. She might even be able to help in some way. "Do you think you could see if Andorra can come over. That way, I can tell you all at once."

"Sure. It sounds…big."

"It kind of is."

"I'll give her a ring." Drake made the call and then faced us. "She'll be right over. What's this about?"

"Time travel and murder," Jaxson said.

He grinned. "Then I came to the right place." He sobered. "Sorry. You were serious. Who died?"

"The skeleton," Jaxson said.

"Bad joke, bro, bad joke. I hardly call that murder—at least not a recent one."

"Maybe not, but just wait until your girlfriend gets here, and we tell you what went down. It gets worse."

Drake held up his hands. "Waiting, but not so patiently."

Thankfully, Andorra must have been at the store, because she arrived a few minutes later, a little out of breath from climbing the stairs. "I came as fast as I could."

"We appreciate it. Have a seat." Jaxson had pulled over the office chairs. If anyone else showed up, we'd have to borrow a few from downstairs.

"I can't wait to hear this," Drake said.

I started with Dominic identifying the skeleton, moved onto Gertrude confessing to the murder, and then how her friend Madam Criant, who we'd met in Ohio, had helped with the deadly spell. I was happy neither asked questions since it would be easier if I went through all of the details.

"Then when Dominic returned after telling Courtney about it, he had a gem with him that she'd given him. Apparently, a worker had found it in the wall of her shop. When he came near me, the gem interacted with my necklace, and all of us time traveled back to Charlotte, Ohio in 1973."

"What?" Andorra asked. That led to a good twenty-minute discussion of that trip. "What are you going to do?"

"That's why I asked you here. I will tell Gertrude what happened, but I'm not sure she's up for the trip—if I can even call it a trip."

"You said you were gone for a day in Ohio yet only a few seconds elapsed here?" Andorra asked.

"Correct."

"Then I'm going with you next time."

Drake clasped her hand. "No. It's too dangerous."

I figured Drake would say that. I wanted to suggest he join us, but there were only so many people who could pass through the portal—or whatever the time travel conduit was called—so many times before it broke down, or maybe I had misunderstood Bethany. Fingers crossed the pathway between times hadn't already died. "She'll be fine."

"Easy for you to say. I'm sure my brother is going with you."

"He is." That's because I relied on Jaxson for not only morale support, but for nixing my crazy ideas. "Let's speak with Gertrude and see what she has to say. We will be doing a lot of séances, and we will need as many witches as we can find."

"Then I'm coming, too," Rihanna said. "And I'm not taking no for an answer. At least this time it won't be so freaking cold."

Maybe I shouldn't be the one who decided who could and couldn't go. "We'll figure it out later. Right now, we need to see what Gertrude has to say."

"I'll stay here," Jaxson said. "Bethany might be trying to come through this time traveling portal as we speak. If she arrives, and we are all gone, it wouldn't be good."

"You're the best." I leaned over and kissed him. "Thank you. Between all of us, we should remember everything. But don't worry. I'm not going without you."

I'm sure Rihanna would have loved to take Gavin, but she probably knew that it would be a bit too much for him.

Before we made the trip for nothing, I called the Psychics Corner to make sure Gertrude was there. She was with a client but would be free shortly, so all but Jaxson headed over. During the walk, I came up with reasons why Gertrude should stay back and reasons why she should come with us. In the end, I'd let her decide.

We only had to wait a few minutes before we were told to go to her office. I suppose I should have warned Gertrude how many would be showing up, but we would find someplace to sit. When I knocked and entered, I had to chuckle at the six chairs around the table. "I hope you just finished with a large group."

She winked. "I'll never tell."

It was fun to pretend she knew everything. I placed Iggy on the table, and then sat at the circular table. Once we were all settled, Gertrude took a seat.

"Tell me what is going on? Besides the fact you snuck back to Ohio to confer with my good friend, Bethany."

My jaw dropped, though I don't know why. She really did know things. "You said we'd get a sign. I thought it would come from Bethany, but she denied it."

I explained about the blue stone and how it interacted

with my necklace. "We ended up in Bethany's store in May of 1973."

"I see. That was about the same time Dominic arrived in Witch's Cove?"

"Yes, ma'am," he said.

"I need to explain why we need to see you." It was possible she knew, but I continued anyway. "I thought that if we could stop Raymond from coming to Witch's Cove, you and Bethany wouldn't need to eliminate him."

I would have been more subtle, but everyone in the room understood what had happened. I explained Iggy's idea of tormenting the man.

"Are you thinking that if Raymond is put away in some mental institution, or is sent to another time, he won't stalk Bethany, and then we wouldn't need to kill him?" Her voice trailed off.

"Yes, and there wouldn't be a skeleton found in Courtney's new shop, which would mean people won't be put off by that event. All around it's a win-win. Okay, maybe not for Raymond, but he did kill a lot of people."

She sat up straighter. "I like it. How do you plan to accomplish this?"

"Iggy came up with a solution. Do you want to give Gertrude the details?" My familiar loved to be the star.

"Sure." He explained about summoning all of the spirits of the dead people and asking them to stay by Raymond's side until they drove him crazy. "He deserves it. We want him to beg for them to stop. Somehow, they'll let him know that if he turns himself in, giving times and dates of the spells and murders, the ghosts will go back to where they live."

"Iggy, you are brilliant," his biggest fan said.

As much as it made me proud to have raised such a smart familiar, he could be a little egotistical at times.

"Aw, shucks," Iggy said.

Really? Did he hear that on an old rerun of some television show? I needed to find out how he knew these things.

"What do I need to do?" Gertrude asked with a lot of enthusiasm.

"Bethany, who was supposed to come back with us didn't for some reason. She said we need to return to Charlotte, Ohio in 1973 in order to do these spells."

Gertrude planted a hand on her chest. "I'll get to see my old friend again if I go with you?"

"Yes." But her old friend would be young. I hope that didn't matter.

# Chapter Fourteen

"I HAVE A question," Gertrude said.

From her serious tone, this might not be good. "Ask away, but no guarantee I'll know the answer."

"Fine. I am aware that you, Iggy, and Rihanna can see and hear ghosts—or rather most of them. Who's to say Raymond will hear those who we summon to drive him mad?"

It felt as if I'd stepped in cement. "I never thought of that. If he can't hear them, it will ruin everything."

Gertrude lifted a hand. "There may be a way to work around that."

I sat up straighter. "What would that be?"

"Remember when your grandmother wrote a note in the steam on your bathroom mirror, even though she had passed?"

"I always believed it was her, but rationally, I know that ghosts can't take a corporeal form."

Gertrude smiled. "Not normally."

My arms tingled. "What are you saying?"

"Your goal is to have these murdered souls mentally torture Raymond until he confesses or commits himself to an asylum, right?"

"Yes." I was glad she understood.

"We will first have to do a spell on these spirits to make

sure that they can be heard by others—specifically Raymond."

"There is a spell? I wouldn't want to go to all this trouble of contacting them and then have it fail."

"Yes, but I want to confer with Levy and his coven to make sure."

It would be too much to hope we could invite Levy to go with us to the past. "No problem."

"What about being able to write him a note like Nana did?" I asked.

"That would require a bit more work, I imagine," she said.

Andorra lifted her hand to signal she wanted to say something. "If I'm Raymond, and I wake up in the middle of the night to people talking to me, I'll think I'm dreaming. Following up to Glinda's comment, is there any way we can have the ghosts leave some evidence that they were there, so that when he wakes up, he'll know it was real and not some dream? It doesn't have to be a written note. They could knock something over."

"I think I've heard of that happening before," Gertrude said.

This was really exciting. Not only could we remove Raymond as a threat permanently, but I'd also learn a lot more about spells and the abilities of ghosts in general.

"Maybe we—and by we, I mean me and Rihanna—can stand outside his bedroom window and listen to what the ghosts are saying." Or was that too dangerous?

"I think it would be a lot safer if Gertrude could locate the spell that will enable a ghost to knock over, say, a vase," Rihanna said.

"I can try to find a spell," Gertrude said.

"I know how," Iggy said.

He'd come up with the plan in the first place, so maybe he did have another good idea. "What's that?"

"If we need to make sure that Raymond hears these ghosts, I could visit him in the next morning and tell him that if he wants the ghosts to stop that he has to turn himself in. If he says, *what ghosts*, then we have a problem."

"I'm never going to let you anywhere near that man. Raymond would put a spell on you in a heartbeat—a spell that could kill you."

"Not if he can't see me." Iggy lifted his upper body. It was either his defiant or proud pose. In this case, he was proud.

Iggy's ability to cloak himself had been very useful in the past. "As far as him understanding what needs to happen on his part to stop the haunting, we could ask each of the ghosts to chant a warning, over and over again, telling him they will only stop if he goes to the police. He can't hurt a dead person."

"Fine." Iggy collapsed onto his stomach in defeat.

"Not to be a downer," Drake said, "but what if Raymond slaps on a pair of noise cancellation headphones, puts on some music, and then falls asleep? He won't hear anything that way."

"That would be bad, but I don't think they had those kinds of headphones in 1973."

He smiled. "I forgot we were time traveling. Continue."

"Drake has a point—not about the earphones—but we need to be able to find out if what we are doing is working," I said. "Iggy mentioned the same issue. How can we be sure

Raymond is receiving the message?"

"We'll know when he turns himself in," Dom said.

"That could take a long time."

"Do you know where Raymond is right now? And by right now, I mean in his time," Gertrude asked. "We can't do anything unless we find him. Just the name of the town is good enough. The ghosts can probably fine tune his location."

I had no idea they possessed such talent. "Not yet, but we have feelers out in the community for his location." I had faith in Sissy.

"Good." Gertrude pulled out her phone. "I'm going to call Bertha and ask her about these spells. As much as I'd like to give Levy time to research, we can't wait forever. If Bertha doesn't know of a spell, I'll go to plan B."

Gertrude stepped over to her desk and pulled out a piece of paper. She then called Bertha and explained about what she was looking for. Andorra's grandmother must have known something, because Gertrude jotted down quite a bit of information.

She hung up and returned. "I have the spell to make sure Raymond can hear the ghosts. Seeing them would take a lot more work, Bertha said. As for them being able to write something on a mirror or knocking over an item? Bertha said that if they are angry enough, they can summon their own energy to do it."

"I've never heard of that," I said. "Of all the ghosts, they would have every right to be the angriest."

Gertrude nodded. "I agree."

I was glad we were all set with the spells then. "I take it we no longer need to find out about Raymond's father and what happened to him?" Going back to convince the mom to leave town had too many flaws.

"That seems so," she said.

"Gertrude, when we go back," Rihanna said, "do we need to take anything with us in order to summon these ghosts—like herbs and stuff?"

I interrupted. "Even if we had bags full of these different spell ingredients, I'm not sure we can carry anything with us. Even that paper Gertrude wrote on might not come with us," I said.

Gertrude sighed. "I wish Bethany were here to answer our questions. She'd know what was available in her town."

"We'll need to memorize what to do then," I said.

"At least I've memorized the names of the people who were murdered, so that's one less thing to remember," Dominic said.

Score one for the winning team. Gertrude passed around the paper with the spells, and I did my best to remember them. I figured between all of us, we could recreate what needed to be done.

"I don't understand why you can't contact the ghosts now," Drake said. "They would have had fifty years to think about what kind of revenge they'd want to take. I'm sure they'd be more than willing and able to find Raymond and bug him to death."

I wish I understood if ghosts had the same emotional thoughts and abilities that we did. "What do you think, Gertrude? Should we do the séances from here and save a trip?"

Gertrude had claimed that the longer a person had been

dead, the harder it was to contact them.

Dominic interrupted. "Even if we do it here, I would have to go back to make sure Raymond turned himself in. Otherwise, how will we know when we succeed?"

"We won't know right away." If Dom was the only one to return to Charlotte, he might not be able to come back, unless Bethany was there. If the worst were to occur, at least Courtney would understand if we told her he sacrificed his future to take down a killer.

Rihanna held up a finger. "When we contact Bethany, we could ask her to do a séance on these people, or rather these ghosts, to warm them up, so to speak. She could find out how willing and able they are to do this. If so, we could work from here."

Bethany had passed a few years ago. "Let's hope the passed-over Bethany can communicate with the Bethany living in 1973."

"Yes, let's hope," Gertrude said.

"We can ask her to find out if Raymond turns himself in. That way Dominic wouldn't have to go back!"

"I like it," Dom said.

How she'd let us know, I don't know, but Bethany would find a way.

Rihanna gathered the candles and placed them on the table. Just as Gertrude was about to light them, someone knocked on her office door, and then Jaxson poked his head in. "Guess who made it?"

Before anyone could say anything, Bethany stepped into the room.

As happy as I was that our time traveler was here, it might

be hard to have a séance with her dead self when her current self is in the room.

All of those thoughts disappeared, though, the moment the two women saw each other, and Bethany literally ran to her friend. I had the feeling that she didn't see an old woman, but rather her best friend from many, many years ago.

Tears welled in my eyes at their joyous reunion. As much as I wanted to solve this issue of Raymond Gonzalez, it did my heart good to see such happiness.

Bethany looked around. "Look at you with your own place. We've both come a long way, my friend."

"We have," Gertrude said. "How was your trip?"

Trip? She hadn't driven here. "Rough. It took me a few tries to make it." Bethany looked over at us. "The portal is wearing thin."

"We thought that might be the case. It was why we were discussing torturing Raymond from here," I said. "It would save on the wear and tear of the portal."

"I don't know if that will work," she said. "I'd feel better dealing with Raymond in the same time zone, so to speak. If we wait a bit, I think we can go back and forth one or two more times. I've heard portals need time to recover."

That made it sound as if they were living, breathing entities. But hey, they might be, for all I knew. "Whatever you think is best. You are the expert."

Bethany huffed. "Considering how much trouble I had getting here, I may have to turn in my title of time traveler extraordinaire." She smiled.

"Bethany might be right about it being more difficult to connect with ghosts from fifty years ago. Don't forget the longer the passage of time since death, the iffier the connection," Gertrude said, reminding us once again.

Jaxson squeezed in two more chairs around the table. Gertrude pushed her chair back. "Take a load off, Bethany, and let me fix you some tea."

For the next few minutes, we let Bethany absorb and enjoy the fact that she had finally done what others had—time traveled—assuming she'd never done it before.

"When Jaxson and I walked over here, I couldn't believe all of the fancy cars. He even showed me his futuristic telephone. It's remarkable." She grinned. "I was so tempted to ask him to jot down a few of today's stock prices for me, but I don't think that would be fair," she chuckled.

I couldn't imagine knowing that much about the future. "No, I guess not."

While I was happy that Bethany Criant had joined us, we had work to do. As I was trying to figure out our next step, the gem on my necklace flashed, causing me to suck in a breath. "Nana?"

"Who's Nana?" Bethany asked.

"My grandmother who passed away many years ago." I explained how she had contacted me several times in the past, and that I was hoping she had some suggestions for us now. "Can we try to contact her?"

"Sure." Gertrude placed Bethany's tea on the table, sat down, and then used the remote to dim the overhead lights before lighting the candles. "Would you like to do the honors, Glinda?"

# Chapter Fifteen

M Y PULSE SOARED at being asked to lead a séance—and for my grandmother no less. The last time we'd contacted Nana, Rihanna had spoken with her. "I'd like that." I looked down at Iggy. "Be ready."

"Gotcha covered."

After all of our hands were connected, I implored my grandmother to tell us if it was even possible for those who had passed to torment the man who'd killed them? I wasn't sure what I expected her to say, but I prayed she would claim it wouldn't be a problem.

As much as I wanted to ask a second question right away, I had to give her time to arrive. She wasn't the promptest person, even when she was alive. It must have been twenty seconds later when Iggy tapped my hand, causing my heart to flutter. Iggy was terrible at keeping his eyes shut, so his silent message implied Nana was here.

When I looked up, a white glow appeared around a floating figure. "Nana?" I choked out.

"Yes, my dear. We don't have much time. Go back to Charlotte. You'll need all of you to contact those who have been wronged. Show them the blue gem. It will let them know the truth and help them do as you desire." And then she just disappeared.

"Wait!" I wanted more guidance, or rather I needed more guidance. How could the blue gem help those who had passed over?

The candle flames flicked, diminished, and then went out. I sank against my chair and drew in my hands.

Rihanna opened her eyes. "I felt her, Glinda."

"I'm sure you did. She was your grandmother, too."

The rest opened their eyes. "What did she say?" Andorra asked.

I told them about the blue gem. "I guess that means if we want to stop this man from following Bethany to Witch's Cove and forcing Gertrude and her to kill Raymond, we have to time travel."

"How does the gem come into play, exactly?" Andorra asked.

"I wish I had the answer to that, but Nana left before she told me. Once we find out where Raymond is staying, we should do a trial run with one of the ghosts. Work out the kinks so to speak."

"That's a good idea," Gertrude said.

"Iggy and I can see him, so maybe we should watch Raymond." I wasn't certain if that was another stupid or dangerous idea.

"I'll come with you when you do," Jaxson said. "If Raymond sees you, he can put a spell on you and kill you."

I thought it obvious that the warlock could kill all three of us, but it would be better to keep my mouth shut for a change. I didn't want to remind Jaxson that he would be powerless against Raymond, too.

"Fine. I wish we could time travel with our cell phones so we could contact you, Bethany, and ask you and the others to summon some ghost reinforcements if need be."

"Me, too, but the other ghosts might rush to your rescue on their own," Bethany said.

"That would be nice, but I won't count on it. When we time travel, nothing comes with us, so I guess there is no need to pack." I'd already said that, but I wanted to make sure everyone understood.

"That's not true," Dominic said. "I had the gem with me when we traveled back in time."

I wonder why the blue gem was an exception. "You did. Since we'll need it for our haunting to work, how about retrieving it and bringing it here."

"Sure."

"I'll go with you." Jaxson said.

"When do you think we should go?" I asked the rest of the group once the two men left.

"Whenever it is, I'm going with everyone," Drake said. "There are people I care most about heading into a dangerous journey. If we never make it back, then so be it."

His passion moved me. Drake was my best male friend. If I was going to spend the rest of my life stuck in Ohio in the 1970s, I wanted him there. "Sounds good. I'm not sure where we will all stay, but we'll find some place."

"Why not stay at the Ashton B&B, assuming there are enough rooms?" Bethany suggested.

"I like that idea." Considering it was summer, Iggy wouldn't need any special outfits to stay warm.

Bethany would be sending us, which meant we'd arrive in

period clothing with the appropriate amount of money and everything else we'd need. I wanted to ask her how in the world she managed that, but I bet she'd say she had no idea what I was talking about.

"I thought I needed to contact Levy," Gertrude said, "but between Bertha and your grandmother helping, we have enough guidance. After all, your Nana is already on the other side. She'll know what to do."

She wasn't on the other side in 1973 though. "That she does." A second later, my pendant heated up once more, making me feel closer to her.

It didn't take Dominic and Jaxson long before they returned with the needed gem. I clasped a hand over my necklace to prevent the two gems from interacting. Bethany then dipped her hand in her pocket. I suspected it was to remove a gold coin to enable our transport. The potion she'd made might have been for show.

Before anyone could ask any last minute questions, we were all once more in her shop.

"It worked," I announced with what I thought was a fairly even and controlled voice. "The question is who did it? Bethany was it your gold coin, or was it the blue gem combined with my necklace?"

"I don't know, and that's the truth."

That could be a problem. I checked to see if Gertrude was okay. She was wearing a rather strange but comfortable-looking muumuu. When she looked around and grinned, I knew she'd arrived none the worse for wear. The fact our clothes were different implied Bethany had been the one responsible for our time travel.

Andorra and Drake seemed frozen for a moment, and I

couldn't blame them. It was the same reaction I'd had the first time I'd traveled back in time.

"How is this possible?" Andorra whispered. "I mean, you said you did this, but to experience it myself is surreal."

"I've learned not to question some things." That was a total lie. I'd pummeled Bethany with questions.

"This is remarkable." Gertrude kept smiling.

"Before we get to work, let me grab a real chair for Gertrude. The beanbag chairs can be hard to get out of." Bethany dragged a chair in from the back room and motioned Gertrude take a seat.

"Thank you. There was no way I was going to get up from down there."

Bethany smiled. "It takes some practice." She sat down. "Okay, as I see it, the first step will be to find Raymond. Not that I want him to be in town, but I know it is our only chance of stopping this man."

"Let's hope Sissy has found out something," I said.

"Who's Sissy?" Drake asked.

"Sissy manages a local diner here. Think of her as the Dolly Andrews of Charlotte, Ohio."

"Diner? What are we waiting for?" Drake said.

That got a laugh out of us. "Bethany, do you think we could ask Sissy right now, even though it's only been a day? Or did more time pass in this period? Ugh. This is so confusing."

"Before we eat, let me call the Ashton B&B and see if they have some rooms. We should settle in and then find Sissy."

I didn't believe for a moment that she didn't know if any rooms were available. I wouldn't be surprised to learn she hadn't had any difficulty getting through the portal but rather stayed behind to make sure we'd have accommodations upon our return. She then probably spent time magically creating suitcases full of our clothes. How she was able to do that I would never understand. The only explanation was that she had to be able to replicate items with her mind.

Bethany counted. "We have four women and three men, but Gertrude you can stay with me. That will get us down to two rooms with an extra cot in each one."

Rihanna, Andorra, and I would share a room, and the brothers and Dominic would take the other one. "Sounds perfect."

She made the call. From the smile on her face, there had been room for us after all. Color me surprised. Not.

"Let's get settled and then go to the diner." Bethany seemed more excited than I'd ever seen her. Being with her best friend probably accounted for a lot of that cheer. "We'll meet back here when you are finished. Then I'll drive Gertrude to my place."

"Sounds good."

The six of us left Bethany's store and headed to the B&B. I swear, Andorra and Drake never stopped smiling.

"This reminds me of Witch's Cove," Andorra said. "It's so freaking quaint."

"It is at that. I like that a lot of the franchises haven't infiltrated the town. Up ahead on your right is Charlotte College."

"It's where I pretended I wanted to attend," Rihanna said. "If I wouldn't miss my family and friends, I would consider coming here."

"I didn't think you liked the cold?"

"I don't, but I can imagine the photo opportunities in the

snow would be awesome," she said.

"You're probably right."

It took less than fifteen minutes to hoof it to the B&B.

"It feels like yesterday that we were here," Jaxson said.

"I know."

Iggy poked his head out from the bag Bethany had lent me and looked around. I thought displaying Iggy in public would result in too many questions. When we arrived at the B&B, who should be there to greet us but Stephanie Carlton, someone we'd met on our last trip. I remembered she'd said she might like to buy the place, but Dominic never said she had.

Stephanie hugged me. "I couldn't believe it when Bethany called and said you were back in town."

It wasn't as if I could say we were time travelers. "Jaxson, Rihanna, and I wanted to see what Charlotte was like in the summer. Trust me, it doesn't disappoint." That was so lame, but I wasn't good at making things up at a moment's notice.

She turned to Dominic. "I'm glad you are here, too, but I thought you'd be back in Washington by now."

"That was the plan until I ran into these guys and thought I'd stay."

I expected Stephanie to ask more questions, but apparently, she didn't care why we were there, just that we were. The fact we'd barely interacted with Dominic six months ago didn't seem to make a difference.

"I'm sure you'll want to freshen up. Give me a sec to grab the keys." She disappeared into her office, the one Mrs. Tully used to occupy. Stephanie returned and handed them to us. "Rooms three and four. I'm sure you know where they are."

"We do."

She looked around. "No luggage?"

"We left it at Madam Criant's since we walked here. She'll drop off all of our stuff later." The lies were compounding.

"Great. Breakfast is served from seven to nine."

"Thanks." I wondered if Bethany's husband, Evan, was still the cook here.

As much as I wanted to ask Stephanie about her daughter and grandkids, I didn't need her asking any more questions about the nature of our trip.

We went upstairs and found our rooms. "Nothing has changed," Iggy said.

"Nope, other than there is a cot in the corner."

Rihanna rushed over to the sofa and looked behind it. "Well, what do you know. Three suitcases."

"There must be a mistake," Andorra said.

"Not a mistake." I had explained what we probably would find inside.

"But how is that possible?" she asked as we carried them over to the bed.

"If I knew the answer to that, I could unlock the mysteries of the universe."

We opened our bags and retrieved what we needed for now. It wasn't long before someone knocked on our door. I answered to find all three men there.

"Ready?" Jaxson asked.

I looked behind me. "Yes."

I would have suggested that Iggy stay behind, but if by some chance we time traveled without meaning to, I didn't want him stuck here. I gathered him up, ready to see if Sissy's sources knew the location of the infamous serial killer.

# Chapter Sixteen

W E WERE ALL seated at the diner, but I didn't see Sissy, and that worried me. "Were we here just yesterday?" I asked.

Keeping track of time had been impossible. Few things seemed to stay consistent between the two eras.

"Yes, we were." Bethany looked around. "Oh, there's Sissy now." She waved to get her attention.

Sissy grinned and rushed over. "You're back."

"We are," Bethany said. "Were you successful in your search?"

"I was. Anna Delaney has a friend in real estate. She told Anna that she'd recently rented a small house out in Crestview, right across the river, to the man you asked about." She stuck her hand in her apron pocket. "Here's the address. I was hoping you'd come back today."

That was impressive work—more than just listening to gossip. Sissy had gone out of her way to find the answer. "You are the best."

"Thanks." Sissy blushed. "So, do you know what you want to order, or do you need more time?"

"Give us a minute," Bethany said.

"Sure." Sissy left to take care of another table.

"Do you know where Crestview is?" I asked as soon as Sissy was out of earshot.

"Yes. Like she said, it's just across the river. I don't know the location of the street, but I have a map. I'll have to do a drive by to be sure which house it is, but it can't be far."

What a shame Google maps hadn't been invented yet. We were spoiled in our century.

"That sounds great. Do we want to do the séances at your shop or at the B&B?" I wasn't sure which would provide more privacy.

"It will be quieter at the shop. How about after I find out which house Raymond is renting, we contact one of the deceased tonight? We'll have to do a spell to make sure Raymond can hear the ghost. I'll also ask them to do a test to demonstrate that a ghost can move a physical object."

"This will be really exciting if we can pull this off," I said.

"It will." Jaxson placed a hand on my arm. "Don't forget, we'll need to rent a car if we plan to monitor him."

"You can go to the car rental place tomorrow," Bethany said. "After dinner, Gertrude and I can try to find the place. It will be light until late. If need be, you can borrow my car when we get back."

"That works."

We picked up our menus. Everything looked good, and by the time Sissy returned, we were ready to order. My stomach was a little jumpy, but I was pretty sure I'd have no problem eating. I ordered a hamburger so that I could remove the lettuce and give it to Iggy.

Halfway through the meal, Drake leaned back. "I think I want to move back to the 70's." He looked over at Andorra.

"You game?" He winked, probably to show he was kidding. Or at least I hoped he was kidding.

"I love this town, but no cell phones and no computers? It would make ordering what I'd need to start a Hex and Bones place a little more difficult."

"Fine. You win." He leaned over and gave her a quick kiss.

If Iggy had seen them smooching, he'd be gagging. I looked at my purse I'd set on the floor and found my familiar sound asleep. Good.

After we were served, had eaten, and paid—leaving a very hefty tip for the work Sissy had done—we walked back to the psychic shop. Since it was still light, Bethany located a map of Crestview.

"I found the street. We shouldn't be gone long. Wish us luck," Bethany said.

I had a feeling that these two psychics never relied on luck, but I said it anyway. "Luck."

Once they left, we discussed which of those who'd been murdered should be contacted first. "Dominic, do you have a gut feeling who would be most receptive?"

"Marie Anderson. She left behind three children. It was the most tragic case."

"Did the FBI ever look into her background. I'm wondering if there was a reason why she needed to return to her past."

He huffed. "Trust me, we had no idea that time travel existed, so we'd have no reason to delve into a murdered victim's past—at least into their distant past."

"That makes sense."

"Does anyone see any paper?" Rihanna asked. "We should jot down Bertha's spells. It will be easier for us to contact the victims if the words are written down."

"You're right. I'll look for something."

I went into the back room expecting to see it filled with occult items. Instead, all it housed was a small kitchen, along with a desk stuffed in the corner. I had to say, I was a bit disappointed. The cabinets above the sink probably contained some herbs or spare candles, but I forced myself not to snoop.

On top of her desk was a stack of paper and a pile of pens. It was almost as if she knew I'd be looking for those particular items. I grabbed a few sheets and a couple of pens and left.

I then doled them out. "Let's write down as much as we can remember and then compare notes."

Rihanna, Andorra, and I would probably do well since we were used to spells. After five minutes, we compared what we'd written, but I never expected Dominic's to be the most complete. "Have you done spells before?"

He laughed. "No, but the FBI trains us how to memorize things."

"That makes sense."

"Now what?" Jaxson asked.

"We should set up two areas since we'll need to do one séance and one spell. The séance is to contact Marie and the other to ensure that Raymond can hear the spirits."

We set about making the table arrangements. Once Bethany and Gertrude returned, we would start.

"After we contact this Marie lady, and Gertrude tells us she's agreed to help, what's the plan?" Jaxson asked.

"What do you suggest? I don't want to put anyone in

jeopardy."

"We'll need to set up a schedule to monitor Raymond. If we assume he goes to bed at midnight, I'm thinking a shift from one to three and another from three to five should do it. What do you all think?"

"Sounds good," Drake said.

"How will we know if we've been successful?" I didn't know why I was so nervous, but I was.

"I imagine we could listen through his bedroom window. If I heard voices, you could rest assured I'd be turning on every light in the house and calling out a few names," Jaxson said.

"Let's do it."

"I'm coming," Iggy said.

I saw no problem with that. He had a lot of hidden talents. "I wouldn't have it any other way."

We were about to practice the spell to make sure Raymond heard the ghosts, when Bethany and Gertrude returned. "We found the house, and I've marked it on the map."

She placed it in front of us and showed us the location. The roads to the home seemed rather straightforward. The house should be easy to find. I explained about our plan, and when we would monitor Raymond.

"Great, shall we get started then?" Bethany said.

Jaxson and Drake were at the séance table since contacting the dead was easier with more people.

"We're ready." I then double-checked that the blue gem still sat in the middle of their table.

We discussed our plan one more time to be sure we were all on the same page. Bethany and Gertrude would summon

Marie. Once she arrived—or rather if she arrived—then Rihanna, Andorra, and I would do the spell to ensure Raymond could hear her. I thought we'd have to do the spell near Raymond, but Bethany explained that it was to enhance Marie's abilities, not his.

With the candles lit and the lights dimmed, Gertrude began by summoning Marie Anderson. "If you could appear in your ghost form, that would be best."

I wasn't aware that those who had died could control their form so easily, but what did I know? Nana always seemed to do the ghost thing, so maybe they could decide which way to communicate.

Everyone at the main table had their eyes closed, but I was watching, as was Iggy. In the far corner, a slight glimmer appeared. I sat up straighter. Iggy dragged a claw across my hand, but it wasn't necessary. I was very aware she was there.

"I see you have the blue gem," Marie said.

"We do." Gertrude explained what we wanted her to do. "Are you willing?"

"More than willing."

"Maybe not tonight, but in the near future, we will endow you with the ability to move physical objects. We want to make this man think he is crazy."

"I know what to do. My anger will guide me." And then she was gone.

I wanted to yell at her not to go, but I'd been to enough séances to know that ghosts didn't really care what you wanted them to do. Andorra nudged me. That's right. It was our turn. I still was uncertain how this worked.

The three of us read the spell, which seemed a bit lame,

but the moment we finished, the blue gem started to glow. "Ladies," I whispered. "Look."

As soon as they lifted their heads, the gem's glow diminished. I waited for Bethany or Gertrude to comment, but both remained fixated on the stone. I thought Bethany might pick it up, but she left it there.

I pushed back my chair and stepped over to their table. "How do you think it went?"

"Well," Gertrude said.

"Did she say anything more to you?"

"No."

Okay, then. If I had a watch, I would have looked at the time. "I guess Jaxson, Iggy, and I are up next."

"Be careful," Bethany said.

"We will be."

She tapped the map where a park was located. "The yellow house is fairly isolated, which is a good thing, but it's two stories, implying the bedroom might be on the top floor."

"That would make it harder to look in," I said.

"I can look in," Iggy said.

Naturally, my first instinct was to protect him, but he might not be in danger. "I suppose it could work. Even if Raymond looked out the window and saw something pink, he wouldn't consider Iggy a threat."

"Yeah, and I can see and hear ghosts!" he announced with pride.

"I say we let him, Glinda," Jaxson said. "When the second shift shows up, Iggy can stay if he likes."

"Works for me, but no talking, Iggy."

"Never."

The group laughed. They understood Iggy had a hard time keeping quiet. "I guess we should head on back to the hotel if we're going to be on lookout duty in a couple of hours," I said.

"Fine by me," Rihanna said.

Since we'd need a car to drive across the river to Raymond's house, we borrowed Bethany's. It was a bit cramped, but we managed to squish in. Good thing it was a short trip.

I doubted I would sleep before midnight, but since my shift was up first, I took the cot and laid down for a quick nap. I swear it wasn't ten seconds later that someone was shaking my shoulder. I opened my eyes to find Jaxson smiling down at me.

He held a finger over his lips and had Iggy cradled in the crux of his arm. "It's time," he whispered.

Yikes, I must have been more tired than I thought. I leveraged my legs over the bed, stretched, and stood. Since I didn't need anything, I followed Jaxson out.

I was in charge of the map while he drove, and I really missed the flashlight app on my cell phone. Finding the switch to turn on the overhead light took some doing, but I managed.

"It should be the next left," I instructed.

He turned down the street. Thankfully, every house had a mailbox with a number on the side, though most were impossible to read in the dark.

"I'll park and casually walk down the street, checking out the numbers." He pulled to the side, and letting the engine idle, got out. "Stay put, Glinda."

Did he think I was going to beep the horn or do a dance

in the middle of the street? It was one in the morning!

It didn't take him long to return. Jaxson slipped into the front seat. "It's that yellow house."

It was pale yellow, which was why I couldn't tell in the dark. "You're up Iggy." I sighed. "I wonder when Marie plans to do her thing? Do ghosts even know what time it is?"

"I'll find out." Iggy crawled off my lap and was out the open window before I could say anything.

I could only hope he didn't mess this up.

# Chapter Seventeen

"NOTHING IS HAPPENING." I was whining, but I was anxious for this to work. It seemed as if we'd been sitting for half an hour at least, even though the dashboard clock said it was closer to five minutes. "What happens if Raymond can't hear Marie?"

"Stop worrying. I have a gut feeling that your grandmother isn't going to let that happen."

"You have a point. She did tell us to come here. I bet if I had my pendant right now, it would be glowing." With that warm thought, I leaned back and waited.

Jaxson nudged me a few minutes later. "Look, there's a light in the upstairs window."

I jerked to attention and sat up. I tried to spot Iggy somewhere near the window, but I couldn't. "Wait. Is that Raymond shouting?"

Jaxson turned his head, as if to listen. "I think it might be."

I grinned. "Is that the sound of a man being tortured?"

Just as I was gloating that we might be succeeding, the front door of the house opened, and I instantly ducked down. We were parked one house away, but we were only one of two cars on the block. As much as it would be wise to leave, we couldn't—not without Iggy.

"Is he coming toward us?" I whispered. Jaxson was still sitting up, his hand on the ignition, ready to start the car.

"Yes," he said quietly.

"What are we going to do? We need Iggy."

I should have a whistle that only my familiar could hear—like a dog whistle, except for lizards. The only problem was that I don't think those existed.

Jaxson started the car, but kept the lights off. Thankfully, he didn't drive away. Just as I was about to ask what we should do, something heavy landed on my lap.

"Go!" Iggy shouted.

I looked down, and he appeared right before my eyes. Jaxson took off.

"That was close," Jaxson said.

"Tell me what happened in there," I asked Iggy.

"It was incredible." If Iggy could have cackled, he would have.

"Meaning?" He was such a drama queen.

"First Marie showed up. I heard her. She was amazing, accusing him of killing her and ruining her family. Then Raymond sat up and looked around. I don't think he could see her, but I could."

"Did he say anything?"

"The usual, like who was there and stuff like that."

"Did he sound scared?" I asked.

"Not at first, but then guess who showed up?"

There were times when I wanted to strangle my familiar. "Tell me."

"Another ghost who knocked something off his

nightstand."

Chills ripped up my body. Had Gertrude and Bethany summoned help, or had Marie called in reinforcements? "Did that freak him out?"

"He jumped out of bed faster than a frog can leap."

I sighed. "I wonder how long it will take before Raymond cracks?"

"Not long, I bet," Iggy said. "He was sounding pretty rattled. He begged her to leave him alone."

"Yes!" I couldn't wait to tell the others that we were on our way to getting rid of Raymond Gonzalez for good.

Before I knew it, Jaxson had parked in front of the B&B. "We need to let Andorra and Drake know that they don't need to keep watch. I think the process has already begun."

"I agree."

WHEN WE ALL walked into Madam Criant's shop the next morning, Gertrude looked up and smiled. What was that about? We hadn't called either of them to let them know what went down. "You look happy," I said.

"We are," Gertrude announced. She then looked over at Rihanna whose face lit up a few seconds later.

"Get out. He went to the cops?" Rihanna asked.

I grabbed Jaxson's hand. "Tell us what you know, and we'll share our story."

Bethany motioned we take a seat. "I called my contact at the sheriff's department, and he told me that a Raymond Gonzalez reported a break-in last night."

A break-in. "Did he say if he caught this elusive thief?"

She laughed. "He tried. They broke in and knocked something off his nightstand, waking him up. He charged after them, but he scared them off."

"I'm curious what he thought the cops could do. Or do you have ghostbusters in town?" I was being silly, but the news was too good not to have fun with it.

"Good thing we don't. Now tell us what you saw," Bethany said.

I gave most of the credit to Iggy. "The item knocked off the table was done by a second ghost."

Gertrude leaned back in her chair and smiled. "This is great. Raymond Gonzalez will be begging to be put away in no time."

"I hope. Anyone want to take any bets on how long it will take for him to crack?" I asked.

"It could take weeks or months," Bethany said. "Because of that, I don't think any of you need to stay."

"You don't need to call on the other ghosts to haunt him?"

Bethany tapped the blue gem that sat on her table. "I have the sense that your Nana sent this to you in order to take care of Raymond. She'll help gather the troops for us. Your grandmother knows how much you care about Gertrude." Bethany smiled. "Someday, she may reveal how she knew to place it in Courtney's shop."

I suppose that could be true. Nana sure seemed to understand its power. "I've been meaning to ask you guys. So, neither of you gave the gem to those men who placed Raymond's body in the wall?"

They shook their heads. "Glinda, to be honest, from the first moment I saw this gem, it's been driving me crazy," Gertrude said. "I, too, want to know where it came from."

"Maybe Nana arranged for us to find it after all." I looked over at Dominic and back at our psychic duo. "Who do you think sent Dominic to us?"

"I would suspect the same person who sent Courtney to Witch's Cove," Gertrude said.

I waited for her to tell me a name. "Nana?"

Bethany shook her head. "When I picked up the gem, I could sense something powerful coming from it. That could mean your grandmother had a hand in it, or it was someone else as powerful or maybe more so."

"The fortune teller from the fair?" That seemed the most likely choice.

"Maybe."

I looked at Dominic. "Did Courtney ever mention anything about her? Like her name?"

"No."

Right now, we probably needed to worry more about Raymond. And Dominic. "Suppose Raymond turns himself in and is committed. He won't follow Bethany, and Bethany and Gertrude won't need to kill him."

"Which means there won't be a skeleton in Courtney's store," Dominic said. "Which means I might not be sent to Witch's Cove in the first place."

Okay, that was a depressing thought. "What do we do?" I looked over at our time-traveling expert.

"You all go home. As in right now, before the future gets written in stone, so to speak."

"I will have to return at some point to make certain Raymond has been put away," Dominic said.

"My dear boy, my contact in the sheriff's department is more than capable of letting me know."

It wasn't fair to ask Drake or Andorra to stay for weeks, and I was sure that Rihanna wanted to get back to Gavin. "Jaxson, what do you think?"

"If Bethany needs us, she can let us know."

She grinned. "Perfect. I'll send you a gold coin with a note inscribed on it if I need anything."

I bet she'd ask for Gertrude to return, but I wasn't ready to let my favorite psychic leave Witch's Cove just yet.

"Are you sure?"

"Yes, and don't worry, I can contact Marie again if need be. She's already contacted the others."

We know she asked one ghost who could move things to help. "Okay then." I was about to ask what our next step should be when all of a sudden, we were back in our Pink Iguana Sleuth's office.

"Are you kidding me?" Andorra said. "Did that really just happen?"

I always had that reaction when I returned. "It did."

"Wait until I tell Elizabeth and Memaw. They are going to be so jealous," Andorra said.

Because they were both so entrenched in the occult, they would probably believe her.

"What about Hugo?" Iggy asked.

Hugo was Andorra's sometime familiar. He mostly took the form of a stone gargoyle, but was human-like when she was in trouble.

"What about him?" she asked.

"Do you think he sensed you were in trouble? I mean, you weren't even, sort of, alive for a few hours. You were back in the 70s."

She looked over at Drake and then at me. "I guess I'll have to ask him."

"Can I come?" Iggy asked. "I miss my friend."

"Maybe later, Iggy. I'm a bit overwhelmed right now," Andorra said.

I picked him up. "Let's let her rest, okay?"

"Fine." He wiggled to get out of my grasp, and I set him down again.

"I, for one, am going to check on Courtney," Dominic said.

"Are you going to see if she found a skeleton in her store?"

"We've only been back, what? Two minutes. I doubt the ghosts were able to drive Raymond crazy in that time."

"Not necessarily true," Jaxson said. "On our last trip, Glinda went through the portal—if that is what we are calling it—days before Rihanna and I did, and yet she thought it was a short period of time."

"I guess I have nothing to lose," Dominic said.

"Can you ask Courtney what town she was in when she had the fortune teller reading? I have an idea, based on what Bethany said."

"What?"

I never liked pretending that I could tell the future. "Ask her first, and then I'll tell you what I was thinking."

"Sure thing, and thanks for another adventure." With that he left the office.

"Andi and I are going to rest," Drake said. "I know it's early in the day, but I feel as if I've been gone a week."

"Who knows? Maybe we have," I said. Drake stilled. "Relax." I picked up my phone off the table and held it out to him. "See? Only an hour has passed."

"If I hadn't just time traveled, I never would have believed it was possible."

Andorra wrapped an arm around his waist. "Welcome to the world of the occult."

After we walked Gertrude back to her place, the three of us headed to the Tiki Hut to grab some food. I think it was around lunchtime, but this going back and forth between different times was messing with my body's rhythm.

"I'll text Dominic and let him know we are at the Tiki Hut. He might want to join us after he has his chat with Courtney," Jaxson said.

"That's assuming he has his cell phone on him."

"We were all dressed in our twenty-first century garb, so I imagine it is business as usual."

"You're right."

I didn't see Aunt Fern at the checkout counter, which meant she was either out and about or upstairs relaxing. I would have to stop over tonight and give her the full rundown. She might have some insight as to who might have sent Courtney here.

Penny looked over, waved, and then motioned we sit in her section. I couldn't wait to tell her all that had transpired. Someday, it would be cool to take her on one of our historic travels.

"I tried calling you a bit ago," Penny said, as soon as we

sat down.

"Jaxson and I were visiting Charlotte, Ohio."

It took a second, but her mouth opened. "You didn't. Why?"

"That discussion will require a bottle of wine."

She smiled. "Gotcha. I can't wait. In the meantime, what can I get you guys to eat?"

Jaxson and I ordered. As soon as she left, I turned to him. "I know this will sound crazy, but I want to find this fortune teller."

"Why?"

"I have this sixth sense that she's related to someone in this town."

"After we eat, I'll do a little research to see if I can find out where that fair is now."

He was the best. "And I want to contact Quade Phillips."

"Bethany's grandson. Why?"

"I know I'm not psychic, but from the way Bethany reacted to the blue gem, I think it could have something to do with this fortune teller. For all we know, it's a relation from a future generation."

He shook his head. "I thought we figured out that your grandmother gave it to you or, rather, sent it to you."

"Bethany thought that might be the case, but she wasn't certain. It's possible someone else is involved in all this mess. Remember, Nana never knew Dominic or Courtney."

He grinned. "You are something else, Glinda Goodall."

I returned his flirty look. "Why is that?"

"Because you never give up, and I admire that."

"Thank you."

I hoped that I wasn't way off course, here, and that it wouldn't take too long to find out the answer.

Our meals arrived and we dug in. Halfway through eating, Jaxson's cell rang. He checked the caller ID. "It's Dominic." He swiped it on. "Hey. What's up?" Jaxson stilled. "You are making that up. Thanks for the intel. Wait until Glinda hears this."

Jaxson disconnected and faced me. "What?"

# Chapter Eighteen

"THE GHOSTS DID their job—or at least I'm assuming they did," Jaxson said.

I didn't want to jump to any conclusions. "Meaning Courtney knew nothing about any skeleton?"

Jaxson smiled. "She never saw one, other than the decorative one sticking out of her wall."

"So much for having to wait for a gold coin with a message on it."

"Don't count Bethany out just yet," he said. "She might be aware that we know that Raymond is safely tucked away and decided not bother sending a coin."

"You're probably right. You know what's going to be weird though?" I asked.

"What?"

"None of the people who checked out Courtney's store to see where the skeleton was found will remember anything." I shook my head. "For as long as I live, I don't think I will ever understand any of the time travel stuff."

Jaxson reached across the table and squeezed my hand. "Don't be so hard on yourself. Bethany doesn't understand all of it either."

"Maybe. Do you think Gertrude will remember even

going to Charlotte?" I asked.

"We remember, so she should too," Jaxson said.

He always was the voice of reason. We finished our meal and then headed back to the office.

Iggy was there. "What's up?" he asked.

He sure seemed to be in a good mood. Aimee must have been impressed with his exploits. "We believe that your plan worked, since Raymond is now in a mental institution."

Iggy did three circles. "Oh, boy. I hope the ghosts never stop haunting him."

I hadn't thought of that. They might not want to stop. "We might have to do another séance and let Bethany know." Or maybe not. The man did destroy a lot of lives.

Jaxson sat down and booted up his computer while I searched through my phone for Quade Phillips' number. It was a long shot, but I had to give it a try.

To my delight, Quade answered on the second ring. "Glinda Goodall. If this isn't a surprise."

"I hope it's a good surprise?" I never knew what to say to him.

"Of course. How can I help you?"

"I just came back from visiting your grandmother."

"Bethany?"

I forgot he probably had two grandmothers. "Yes."

"How is she?"

"Great." I spent the next ten minutes explaining the reason for the trip. "Here's the thing. When she touched the blue gem, she got a familiar reading off of it. It could be because my deceased grandmother had sent it—though they'd never met—or it might have come from another source. Do you have any relatives in the psychic field?"

He didn't answer for a moment. "My sister, Emily."

My heart fluttered. "She's a psychic like her grandmother?"

"My sister claims she is a fortune teller."

Blood pumped hard through my veins. "Where does she live?"

His laugh came out rueful. "She doesn't live anywhere, but it's not like our dad isn't willing to give her whatever she wants. Emily just yearns for a free lifestyle. She actually travels with a local fair, going from town to town."

"Do you know where she is now?"

"I'm sorry, I don't. Emily doesn't reach out very often."

"That's such a shame." It really was. "Do you have her phone number by any chance or her email address?"

"She doesn't own a phone, but she borrows one from a friend from time to time and checks in. Computers are evil, or so she says."

I couldn't live without mine. "If she calls you, could you have her contact me? She might have been the fortune teller who told my friend to come to Witch's Cove. It's a long shot, I know."

"I most certainly will." He then disconnected.

"Well?" Jaxson asked. "What did Quade say?"

I gave him the low down. "Did you ask Dominic where Courtney had her fortune teller reading?"

"Nope, I forgot." He called Dominic back and asked him. "Seriously? In Hilltop, Ohio?" Jaxson looked over at me with wide eyes. "That's where Raymond is from. What are the odds?" Jaxson opened his mouth. "Okay, see you soon."

I could put the pieces together. "Courtney and Raymond being from the same town is no coincidence."

"I have to agree with you, but fifty years is a long time. They wouldn't have personally met."

"No, indeed," Jaxson said.

"We really need to find out where the fair is now." It was another long shot, but Jaxson was talented.

"Give me a moment."

A few minutes later, Dominic stopped in the office. "Guys."

"Hey, Dominic," I said. "Did you tell Courtney where you were recently?"

"I did."

"Did she believe you? If she had no idea she'd had a skeleton in her wall, she might have not remembered you could time travel."

"Thankfully, the only thing she didn't know about was Raymond Gonzalez's body."

"That's great."

"I'm still speechless that Courtney and Raymond are from the same hometown. Is that a coincidence or what?"

"I'd like to find that out." I explained how we were trying to track down the fortune teller.

"You think she'll know why she suggested Courtney move to Florida? Courtney picked Witch's Cove, not this psychic."

"I know, but Emily—if that is her name—might have put the idea into Courtney's head."

"And does this Emily chick believe that I'd be the perfect man for her?" he asked.

"Not that you aren't perfect, but I imagine there are other

men in our time who would suit her. That's why I'm thinking Raymond Gonzalez is connected to all of this somehow. She needed Courtney to say a love spell at the same time you wished for a girlfriend. That would bring you here. You are the only person who would have been able to identify Raymond Gonzalez."

"I can see where this is headed. Either the fortune teller or your grandmother sent the blue gem that transported us back in time where we changed the past. That prevented both Bethany and Gertrude from having to kill someone."

"Right. In the end, not only do you and Courtney have a happily ever after but so do Gertrude and Bethany."

His eyes lit up. "That means this fortune teller is probably related to Courtney, Bethany, or Gertrude."

"That was my thought."

"Glinda, if you could be in two places at once, you would fit the bill since you're connected to all three," he said.

"But I can't time travel anyone, so no, it wasn't me. I'm hoping your research will show us the way."

Jaxson smiled. "We'll see."

Since he needed to learn his way around the Internet, Dominic sat next to Jaxson.

"Dom, do you recall when Courtney came to town?" Jaxson asked.

"Not the exact date, but I can call her."

"Great. More specifically, we need to know when she went to the fair where the fortune teller told her to come to Florida," he said.

Dominic pulled out his phone, adeptly navigated his way to his contacts, and called her. As soon as she picked up, he grinned. "Hey. Sorry to bother you, but Glinda and Jaxson are trying to track down the fortune teller that told you to come here. She thinks the psychic might be related to someone we know. Do you remember when you went to the fair? Sure, I'll wait." He covered the phone. "She's looking at her calendar. "July 3rd? Great. Thanks. Have fun tonight."

Aw, they were so sweet together.

"It should be fairly easy to cross reference that date since we know the fair was in Hilltop, Ohio, at the time," Jaxson told Dominic.

Jaxson explained about Google search and which link might give him the answers. It took longer than what I wanted, but eventually Jaxson found the fair site and dates. He scanned the list and then shook his head.

I stepped behind him. "What is it?"

"The universe is definitely telling us something."

"What?" Iggy crawled up my leg and sat on my shoulder. Even he could tell something big had happened.

"The next fair opens on Saturday in, get this, Charlotte, Ohio."

Words left me. "Seriously?"

He tapped the screen. "Seriously."

"You know, it might be fun to go there and see how the town has changed. I know Bethany will have passed, but we could find her granddaughter."

"What if she isn't the fortune teller?"

I almost rolled my eyes. "Come on. Quade said his sister was one and traveled with a fair. The fact it is going to be in Charlotte has to mean something."

He turned around in his chair and grabbed me around the

waist. "Is that your way of asking me to go with you?"

I almost jumped up and down. "Yes. We've been wanting to have a little vacation. We'll only stay a day or two. We don't want to miss Courtney's grand opening."

"No, we can't miss that." Jaxson turned to Dominic. "You're welcome to join us."

He held up a hand. "I think it will be better if I don't go back there. My luck, I'd be swept back in some vortex of time."

While I didn't think that was even possible, I don't blame him for wanting to be cautious. Besides, he'd much rather help Courtney here. "We'll text you with what we find out."

"Sounds wonderful. But if we are going to make it in time, we'll have to fly out tomorrow," I said.

Jaxson grinned. "I'm on it, pink lady."

"IT LOOKS SO festive," I said to Jaxson. This fair had a Ferris wheel, two rollercoasters, a fun house, and about ten other rides, not to mention a petting zoo. "I really want some cotton candy, and of course, fudge, but I realize we are here to find Emily."

"Very true," Jaxson said.

"Now I'm sorry that we didn't bring Iggy with us."

"He'll get over it, assuming we buy him something."

He wasn't into toys, but there had to be something he'd like. Maybe, I'd promise him a hibiscus plant just for him. I could have a real plant behind the Tiki Hut restaurant and another one by our office.

We walked around for a bit until we finally asked for help in finding the fortune teller.

"Sure, Emily is through that door. You'll find her on the left hand side," one of the workers said.

Chills raced up my arms at the mention of her name. "Thanks." I turned to Jaxson. "I can't believe I'm nervous. Should I tell her I've met her brother and knew her grandmother?"

"Maybe stick with the grandmother part."

"Do you think she'll believe we time traveled fifty years?" I asked.

Jaxson wrapped a secure arm around my waist. "The only way to find out is to mention it to her."

I nodded. "You're right."

We entered the large tent where there were jugglers, clowns, and a slew of other people. At the end of the row on the right was a sign that announced, Madam Phillips. I had to smile. That reminded me so much of her grandmother.

No one was inside with her, so we entered. She looked and smiled. "Welcome." Then she stilled as if she was getting a reading off of us. "I like your necklace. Where did you get it?"

It pulsed twice. Holy moly, was Nana communicating with Emily? "My grandmother left it to me when she passed."

"I'm sorry. It's beautiful."

"Thank you." I had so much I wanted to say, but the words kept jumbling up in my head.

"Have a seat." She pointed to the prices of a reading. "Is that okay?"

"Yes, but we really came here to ask about a Courtney

Higgins."

She shook her head. "I don't know her."

Sure, she didn't. "Okay, here's the bottom line. Whether you believe us or not is up to you. I am a witch." From there I explained about Raymond Gonzalez and how he stalked Emily's grandmother, Bethany, and how she was so desperate to stop him that she and her friend, Gertrude, did a spell that killed him.

I expected her to laugh or call me names. Slowly, her mouth opened. "Did it work?"

"Did what work?"

"Did Courtney fall in love with Dominic?"

I chuckled. She knew. "I think they are on their way."

"And my grandmother. You really saw her?"

That began a very long tale that involved many time crossings. "Can I ask you about the blue gem that we found in the wall where Raymond Gonzalez died. Well, he didn't end up dying there since we changed time."

She laughed. "Yes, it was me, but I had help."

"Did you hire one of Courtney's workers to put it there?"

Her brows scrunched. "No, Amelia, your grandmother, helped."

She could have blown me over with a feather. "How?"

Emily shrugged. "I don't know. She came to me in a dream and told me what I needed to do."

"Wow." This was surreal. We chatted a bit more, until another couple came for a reading. I slapped my thighs. "I can't thank you enough for talking to us and for clearing up so many things."

"For me too. I loved my Grammy. You are so lucky.

What I wouldn't give to be able to see her one more time."

Don't ask me why I looked down, but I did. On the ground was a gold coin. My breath hitched as I bent down to pick it up.

On the coin was written the word: Emily.

# Chapter Nineteen

"I STILL CAN'T believe that Bethany sent her granddaughter a coin," I said to Jaxson. We'd returned from Ohio two days ago and were getting ready for Courtney's grand opening.

"Even more amazing was that she believed you when you told her she could visit her grandmother with it," Jaxson said.

"I know, right? What I wouldn't give to be a fly on the wall and watch that reunion."

He chuckled. "Be careful what you wish for. Remember, what happened the first time you made a wish."

Boy, did I. I wished for a white Christmas and got a whole heck of a lot more than that. I straightened my necklace. "Ready to celebrate Courtney's opening?"

"You bet."

"Can I come?" Iggy asked.

"There will be a lot of people, and you might get squished."

"I'll be careful."

I worried that some people might be put off with an iguana wandering around where food was served. "There might be some kissing."

"Then forget it."

I had to work hard not to laugh. I motioned with my

head that we needed to leave before Iggy changed his mind. When we stepped outside, I was surprised by the large number of people in the streets.

"Do you think they are all for Courtney's Broomsticks and Gumdrops opening?" I asked.

"Let's find out," he said.

We walked across the street, and actually had a hard time getting into the store. The place was jammed, and I couldn't be happier.

I leaned my head toward Jaxson. "Dominic is working the cash register?"

"Yeah. Courtney asked him if he could help out. She figured she'd be working with the customers."

I knew Rihanna had said she'd help out behind the soda counter, but I never expected her boyfriend to be beside her. There were six stools, but only three were taken, so Jaxson and I slipped next to Steve.

"Hey, there," he said. "I figured you'd show up sooner or later."

"I can't stay away from candy."

Rihanna rushed over. "A chocolate shake?"

"You know me too well."

She looked over at Jaxson. "Since this is a special occasion, I'll have the same," he said.

Rihanna grinned. "You got it."

"So, Glinda, what have you been up to? We haven't had a case together in weeks," Steve said.

I was about to ask him what he was talking about until it occurred to me that we wouldn't have worked together since there had been no skeleton. If I ever questioned whether messing with the past could affect things, I had my answer. "Just taking long walks on the beach and enjoying the sunsets. Because we had some time, Jaxson and I even took a small vacation."

"That's awesome. Good for you."

Courtney came over and tapped me on the shoulder. "Thanks for coming."

"I wouldn't miss it for the world. This place is going to be a huge success. I can feel it."

"Thanks. I had so many compliments on the skeleton. That was a great suggestion."

"You're welcome."

She handed me a small, white bag. "This is a token of my appreciation for all you have done."

"I haven't done much." Unless Courtney believed Dominic that there had been a skeleton, and I had helped change the present. All I know is that she had come to Witch's Cove and had found love.

I shook the bag slightly. "What is it?"

"Open it."

I looked inside. "Are you kidding? Pink gumdrops? I love it." I leaned up and gave her a hug.

"You're welcome." Dominic called her name. "Oh, I have to see what he needs. Excuse me."

"No problem. Go."

"Here are your drinks," Rihanna said. "Ah, what's this?"

I looked down and spotted a gold coin. "Oh, no. Don't touch it."

"But there's writing on it."

Both Jaxson and I leaned over it, and then I smiled. "It's

from Bethany. She says, thank you."

"Do you think that means that her granddaughter made it back?" Rihanna asked.

"It means whatever we want it to mean. Right now, I am going to enjoy this chocolate shake with some people that I love."

I hope you enjoyed Broomsticks and Pink Gumdrops. I don't know what it is about time travel, but it fascinates me. Charlotte, Ohio is a town based on my college town in Ohio. I haven't been back since then, but I have a trip planned soon. Trust me, I intend to fly there, not time travel, but if I could do it that way, I would.

What's next? KNOTTED UP IN PINK YARN is the story of a new store owner of the former yarn shop. Only this owner has a major agenda that ends up with someone dead. My favorite part? A gargoyle gets to help solve the mystery.

Buy on Amazon or read for FREE on Kindle Unlimited

*Don't forget to sign up for my Cozy Mystery* newsletter *to learn about my discounts and upcoming releases. If you prefer to only receive notices regarding my releases, follow me on BookBub.*
http://smarturl.it/VellaDayNL
bookbub.com/authors/vella-day

Here is a sneak peak of book 13: Knotted up in Pink Yarn

MY BEST FRIEND, Penny, rushed into my apartment carrying a bottle of red wine, waving a small bag, the scent of something spicy wafting behind her. Cookies, perhaps? Or was she trying out a new perfume? She was wearing more make-up than usual. Hmm. Maybe she'd come from visiting her boyfriend.

"You have to see what I made you." She was panting, because the stairs up to my place were rather long and steep.

"What did you bring me?" I couldn't remember when Penny had ever made me anything, but I was excited nonetheless. I took the proffered bottle of wine and set it on the scarred, wooden coffee table that would have to be replaced one of these days. "I'll get us some glasses. It seems like forever since we've had a girls' night."

"Tell me about it." She sat down on the sofa and patted the seat cushion next to her, signaling Iggy to join her.

No surprise, my pink iguana rushed over to her. He loved Penny probably because she always told him how smart he was. I quickly retrieved the corkscrew, grabbed two wine glasses that had been through the dishwasher one too many times, and returned to the living room.

I plopped down next to my friend and placed our celebration items on the coffee table. She understood it was her job to open the wine since she was really good at using the corkscrew. Only then did I notice the label on the bottle. It was the wine my grandmother used to drink, and my heart warmed. Nana always had a glass before dinner, claiming it calmed her soul.

But enough reminiscing. I didn't want to tear up or Penny would think something bad had happened—which it hadn't. Of late, though, I had been missing my grandmother more than ever, probably because she'd come to me in her ghostly form quite a lot lately. I cleared my throat. "Can I open my present now?"

"Absolutely. I just finished it yesterday."

It? Not them, as in a dozen cookies? I wasn't aware that Penny was the arts and crafts type, though she'd surprised me in the past, like when she made her waitressing costume. My aunt, who as the owner, insisted we wear a costume to work at the Tiki Hut Grill. No surprise, Penny had sewn pennies all over her skirt that made her outfit a bit noisy but cute. It was quite clever and always a hit with the customers. I used to dress up as Glinda the Good Witch, in part because I liked wearing pink, and in part because my name is Glinda. My magic wand that doubled as a pencil could be purchased in the gift store.

Penny might not have changed all that much in the last four years since we became friends, but I had. I was no longer waitressing with her at my aunt's restaurant. Instead, I was now running my own business, the Pink Iguana Sleuths with my boyfriend, Jaxson Harrison—something I swore I never wanted or rather would never have. And I'm talking about not wanting or having a boyfriend. I'd always dreamed of running my own business.

As for Jaxson, I'm glad I didn't stick to my rule of being totally independent. He was the best thing to come into my life. Thanks to his influence, as well as my cousin, Rihanna's, I was branching out in the wardrobe department, too. While I always wore my signature pink somewhere, that color no longer dominated my entire look. I was actually wearing blue jeans right now. Okay, I had on pink sneakers, but my white t-shirt should count for something.

I picked up the rather small papered gift bag, opened it, and looked inside. No smell floated upward, so it wasn't cookies. Darn. With the wad of white tissue paper on top of the gift, I couldn't tell what was inside. I stuck my hand in and pulled out a soft, squishy item that I couldn't identify.

"Hmm." I flipped it over, but it looked the same from both sides. It was some sort of knitted pink and green *thing*. It was about four inches wide and maybe eight inches long. "Is it a potholder?"

She laughed as she uncorked the bottle of Merlot. "No, silly. Look at the two loops on one end and the buttons on the other."

That didn't clear up anything. I huffed out a laugh. "Of course, it's a beer cozy." I rarely drank beer, but maybe it was for Jaxson when he came over. Though I'd never seen an eight-inch tall beer can before.

Hmm. The stitches were a little uneven, implying this might have been Penny's first knitting attempt.

She rolled her eyes as she uncorked the wine. "No. Give it to me. I'll show you."

Once she finished pouring the two glasses, she handed me my drink. Penny then adjusted Iggy on her lap and wrapped the coaster-thingy around his body, buttoning it in place. "It's a sweater for Iggy. You know how cold he gets in the winter."

It was July, but I didn't think it wise to mention that fact. "It fits him perfectly." Or it kind of did. It might even stay on as long as he didn't move too fast. "What do you say, Iggy?"

Iggy wiggled his body and then looked up at Penny. "Thank you. I love it."

And yes, my iguana could talk. I am a witch, after all, and Iggy is my familiar.

Penny grinned. "See? I knew you would. Glinda, you have to come with me to the yarn shop Sunday for our knitting circle. You could make all sorts of things for Iggy."

Oh, joy. "That's okay. I'm not really the knitting type." That being said, I did love the feel of the soft wool, the brilliant colors, and the soothing clacking of the needles, but who had time for that? Even if Jaxson and I weren't working on a case, if I had some spare time, I'd rather be reading a book.

"Do you think I am the artsy type?"

"Not all the time, so why did you really go there?" Something was going on with her.

"Hello! The gossip."

"We get plenty of gossip from the ladies." My aunt being one of the biggest participants. Okay, Dolly Andrews, the owner of the Spellbound Diner might be the biggest gossip queen in town, though in truth, she learned most of her news from the sheriff's grandmother, Pearl Dillsmith. "Maybe I should ask you who is in this knitting group of yours?"

Penny already had a hunky boyfriend, so it wasn't as if she was looking to find someone—not that I'd expect many men to show up, but you never know.

"I've only been twice, and both times, different women have been there. Have you met the new owner yet?"

Was she avoiding answering my question for a reason? "No, but I heard she's French."

Penny shook her head and then sipped her wine. "She just likes people to think that. While I could detect a bit of an accent, I think it might be fake. The shop is covered in French artifacts, though. She has a three foot tall replica of the Eiffel Tower, basket fulls of plastic baguettes, a pile of empty wine bottles next to plates of fake cheese, and some random statues. One is Rodin's Thinker. It makes sense, I guess, since her name is Fifi LaRue." Penny rolled her eyes.

I knew her name, but that was all. "I have no room to talk about funny names." In case it wasn't obvious, I was named after a witch in *The Wizard of Oz*. "Fifi LaRue does seem a little made up to me."

"Right? Fifi is better suited for a dog than a person."

I chuckled and then sipped my wine. Oh, yum. The smooth oak flavor slid down my throat. Go Nana. She had good taste in wine, and now apparently so did Penny. "Exactly. I would have thought Lulu, Cheri, Angelique, or even Juliette would better suited as a name. Those scream authentic France just as much if not more so than Fifi. I'll ask Jaxson to do a little digging on her. You said you didn't get the sense she was on the up and up. Was it because her accent sounded fake?" Or was it more than that?

Penny was my human lie detector. Being a witch, she had talents above and beyond others. It was just a shame that she didn't work on polishing her magical skills. "Maybe."

"Did she say why she decided to settle in Witch's Cove and use a fake name—assuming it is fake."

"I guess everyone has the right to be whomever they want, though I sensed something is off, which is why I want to keep going. She's different, I'll tell you that." Penny sipped her wine, and then closed her eyes for a moment, clearing enjoying the full-bodied flavor.

"Different how?" I asked.

She pressed her lips together. "I can't quite put my finger on it, but she seems angry and a bit ill at ease around people."

"Most shop owners are very outgoing. What do you know about her, other than she seems to love knitting and France?"

"She's likes to talk, which is probably why she started the knitting circle."

"Liking to talk and being ill at ease around people don't seem to go together." I'd yet to stop in the new store, aptly named, *Fifi's Yarns*. Clearly, I needed to go sooner rather than later. I loved mysteries.

"I should have said, she'll chat about what she wants to talk about. I don't get the sense she is a good listener."

That could be said about a lot of people. Iggy pawed at the sweater, probably because he was overheating. "Come here, Iggy. We don't want to ruin the sweater before winter."

"Yeah. I don't want to get it dirty." If he could roll his eyes, he would be doing just that.

I removed his wrapper—a name that seemed more appropriate than sweater since the yarn didn't cover his legs. "I don't know why I haven't stopped over at the shop yet and welcomed her to Witch's Cove, but we were kind of busy trying to correct something that went wrong in the past at the candy store." Like a dead body being stuffed in the wall.

"You mean your trip to Ohio?"

"Yup." That had been another night of popcorn, wine, and much candy to get through that story. "So, what else can you tell me about this Fifi woman."

"She's very put together in a French aristocratic sort of way. I'd say she's probably in her late thirties and is very pretty. Here's the thing. The owner seems both angry and unhappy. I think it could be because she was recently divorced."

"That would make anyone upset or depressed. Do we know where she is from?"

"Somewhere near the Florida Panhandle, I think, but I can't be sure. I was concentrating on trying to make my stitches even that I didn't catch all of the facts. If you look closely, you'll see I wasn't all that successful at keeping things in a straight line."

"It's the thought that counts. It is sweet of you to think of my familiar."

"I swear some of the women don't even need to look at what they are doing, and their rows come out perfect."

It was as if she hadn't heard a word I'd said. "I'm sure it's a matter of practice. What are you working on next?"

"A cap for Tommy. I'll have to ask Fifi to help me with using the round needles, if that is what they are called, since some of the women said they are hard to use. Worse case, I can watch a video on the Internet. You can learn everything that way."

I wish I could learn how to do fool-proof spells. "You are right."

"I realize it's still summer, but winter will be here before we know it, and I want Tommy to be warm."

Winter. Ugh. I shivered at that thought. Sure, it was Florida, but sometimes the cold wind would whip off the ocean like a stone skipping across the pond and chill me to the bone. "Tell me again who is in your group."

"There were five of us the first time I went. One or two were new to me. I did get the name of one woman. It was Genevieve Dubois."

I smiled. "Ooh. I like her name. Is she French, too?"

"I don't know. She doesn't have an accent. She seems sweet, though. I don't think she's ever knitted before either, because she's actually a worse knitter than me." Penny smiled.

Wait until I showed up. "Interesting. Where is she from?"

"I didn't ask," Penny said.

Really? Why not? Penny was not shy. Oh, well, to each her own, I guess. I had no such qualms asking fairly personal questions. "While I don't want to look like a fool and show everyone that I don't have a clue how to knit, I might have to put my pride aside and join you all. I love meeting new people and trying to figure them out."

She chuckled. "You just like to psychoanalyze them."

"Nothing's wrong with that." I might have majored in math, but I found people intriguing. And complicated. And sometimes not what they seemed.

After Penny finished telling me who else was in her knitting circle, we talked about how it was going between her and her beau, Hunter Ashwell.

She sighed. "I'm in love."

"Oh, Penny, I am so happy for you. I hope Hunter feels

the same way." I bet her new makeup and enticing new scent were due to Hunter.

"He hasn't said. I believe it's because he thinks his ability to shift into a wolf will eventually turn me off, but that's not going to happen. Besides, it's not as if I haven't seen him in both his animal and human form before, and I'm totally fine with it."

"Be honest. We were both a bit freaked out the first time we saw men shift."

"True, but I've had time to get used to it. Maybe when Tommy gets a bit older, we'll tell him, and then Hunter will feel comfortable enough to tell me how he feels."

"That makes sense, but you should talk to him," I said. "Most men aren't good at reading people. Tell him that you accept him for what, or rather who he is. It's not like he had a choice whether to be a werewolf or not."

She huffed out a laugh. "I know, but I'm not in a hurry. However, you're not one to talk. It's not like you've told Jaxson exactly how you feel."

"He knows I love him, though I haven't said those three little words to him yet. When we took that three-day vacation to the Florida Keys, I think I made it clear that I loved being with him. Actions always speak louder than words, right? At least, that is what both my mother and her mother used to say."

"Has he hinted at marriage?"

For some unknown reason, chills raced up my arms just as my pink pendant heated up. I stilled. Was my grandmother trying to tell me to go for it, or was she remembering how we used to talk for hours about my dreams? "Not yet, but I'm not in a rush."

"You're twenty-seven. Times a ticking."

I laughed. "You sound like my mother. And besides, you're no youngster." She was almost thirty-four.

Penny grinned. "It's not like I need any more kids. Tommy is enough to handle."

Her eight-year-old was rambunctious for sure. Since we were discussing love lives, we went on to talk about how well the new candy store owner, Courtney Higgins, and her time-traveling new boyfriend, Dominic Geno, were getting along.

"Her store is doing well, too," Penny said. "I think having the kids out for the summer is really helping her sales. Every time I walk by, there are people at the soda counter, too."

Her shop had every kind of candy imaginable. My mother said there was candy from when she was young. "When the tourists come in the winter, she'll do even better."

"I'm sure, and it doesn't hurt that Courtney is pretty, bubbly, and a good businesswoman. With Dominic by her side, she can't go wrong," Penny said.

"You are so right."

We finished off our wine, chatting about everything under the sun, including my lack of clients. I guess since Jaxson and I weren't trained in the traditional sense to be private investigators, we couldn't complain that we didn't have people waiting in line for our services. Most of the time we ended up helping the sheriff with one of his cases, especially if magic was involved. Thank goodness, we'd come into a large sum of money a few cases back, or we would have to return to our old jobs.

She yawned, and then stood. "This has been so much fun,

but I've gotta go. Mom is babysitting Tommy, and I have the early shift tomorrow."

"I can still remember those days when I had to drag my-self out of bed at six in the morning to serve breakfast at the restaurant." I hugged Penny goodbye and walked her to the door. "Later."

"We must do this again soon."

"Totally."

As soon as she left, a sense of malaise washed over me. I never realized how much I loved being around people. Now that we had no cases to work on, I was kind of lost. Yes, I had Jaxson, but he had a life, too.

Iggy crawled over to the door and looked up at me. "Do I have to wear that sweater thing?"

"I thought you loved it."

"It's pink."

Poor Iggy. "And half green. I really appreciate you telling Penny you liked it, though, but what's wrong with pink? You're pink."

"Oh, how the irony escapes you."

I cracked up. Iggy always could make me smile.

BUY ON AMAZON OR READ FOR FREE WITH
KINDLE UNLIMITED

THE END

**A WITCH'S COVE MYSTERY** (Paranormal Cozy Mystery)
PINK Is The New Black (book 1)
A PINK Potion Gone Wrong (book 2)
The Mystery of the PINK Aura (book 3)
Box Set (books 1-3)
Sleuthing In The PINK (book 4)
Not in The PINK (book 5)
Gone in the PINK of an Eye (book 6)
Box Set (books 4-6)
The PINK Pumpkin Party (book 7)
Mistletoe with a PINK Bow (book 8)
The Magical PINK Pendant (book 9)
The Poisoned PINK Punch (book 10)
PINK Smoke and Mirrors (book 11)
Broomsticks and PINK Gumdrops (book 12)
Knotted Up In PINK Yarn (book 13)
Ghosts and PINK Candles (book 14)
Pilfered Pink Pearls (book 15)

**SILVER LAKE SERIES (3 OF THEM)**
**(1). HIDDEN REALMS OF SILVER LAKE**
(Paranormal Romance)
Awakened By Flames (book 1)
Seduced By Flames (book 2)
Kissed By Flames (book 3)
Destiny In Flames (book 4)
Box Set (books 1-4)
Passionate Flames (book 5)
Ignited By Flames (book 6)
Touched By Flames (book 7)

Box Set (books 5-7)

Bound By Flames (book 8)

Fueled By Flames (book 9)

Scorched By Flames (book 10)

## (2). **FOUR SISTERS OF FATE: HIDDEN REALMS OF SILVER LAKE** (Paranormal Romance)

Poppy (book 1)

Primrose (book 2)

Acacia (book 3)

Magnolia (book 4)

Box Set (books 1-4)

Jace (book 5)

Tanner (book 6)

## (3). **WERES AND WITCHES OF SILVER LAKE**

(Paranormal Romance)

A Magical Shift (book 1)

Catching Her Bear (book 2)

Surge of Magic (book 3)

The Bear's Forbidden Wolf (book 4)

Her Reluctant Bear (book 5)

Freeing His Tiger (book 6)

Protecting His Wolf (book 7)

Waking His Bear (book 8)

Melting Her Wolf's Heart (book 9)

Her Wolf's Guarded Heart (book 10)

His Rogue Bear (book 11)

Box Set (books 1-4)

Box Set (books 5-8)

Reawakening Their Bears (book 12)

## ROCK HARD, MONTANA
(contemporary romance novellas)
Montana Desire (book 1)
Awakening Passions (book 2)

## PLEDGED TO PROTECT
(contemporary romantic suspense)
From Panic To Passion (book 1)
From Danger To Desire (book 2)
From Terror To Temptation (book 3)
Pledged To Protect Box Set (books 1-3)

## BURIED SERIES (contemporary romantic suspense)
Buried Alive (book 1)
Buried Secrets (book 2)
Buried Deep (book 3)
The Buried Series Complete Box Set (books 1-3)

## A NASH MYSTERY (Contemporary Romance)
Sidearms and Silk(book 1)
Black Ops and Lingerie(book 2)
A Nash Mystery Box Set (books 1-2)

## STARTER SETS (Romance)
Contemporary
Paranormal

# Author Bio

Love it HOT and STEAMY? Sign up for my newsletter and receive MONTANA DESIRE for FREE. smarturl.it/o4cz93?IQid=MLite

OR Are you a fan of quirky PARANORMAL COZY MYSTERIES? Sign up for this newsletter. smarturl.it/CozyNL

Not only do I love to read, write, and dream, I'm an extrovert. I enjoy being around people and am always trying to understand what makes them tick. Not only must my romance books have a happily ever after, I need characters I can relate to. My men are wonderful, dynamic, smart, strong, and the best lovers in the world (of course).

My Paranormal Cozy Mysteries are where I let my imagination run wild with witches and a talking pink iguana who believes he's a real sleuth.

I believe I am the luckiest woman. I do what I love and I have a wonderful, supportive husband, who happens to be hot!

# Fun facts about me

(1) I'm a math nerd who loves spreadsheets. Give me numbers and I'll find a pattern.

(2) I live on a Costa Rica beach!

(3) I also like to exercise. Yes, I know I'm odd.

I love hearing from readers either on FB or via email (hint, hint).

## Social Media Sites

**Website:** www.velladay.com
**FB:** facebook.com/vella.day.90
**Twitter:** @velladay4
**Gmail:** velladayauthor@gmail.com

Printed in Great Britain
by Amazon